哈福

哈福

·跟美國人學·
食衣住行美語會話
Everyday English

專為英語單字不多，立志講一口純正英語的人編寫

（ 真正會講英語的人，使用的單字不多
不須再學三年五載，才能開口說英語 ）

美國人都是這樣說英語的

OK!

What time of day?
（那一天幾點？）

That won't do.
（那不行！）

SCAN

附QR 碼線上音檔
行動學習 即刷即聽

施孝昌 ◎著

哈福

觀光旅遊、移民生活、
留學遊學，看這本就夠了

　　食衣住行美語會話，Everyday English，超簡單、超好學，每一句都是通行全世界的英語，就從今日開始，開口說流利的美語！

　　真正會講英語的人，使用的單字不多。經典著作《狄克森成語》的作者狄克森先生有句名言：「說英語只要300個單字就夠了。」講流利的英語，原本就不需要太多的英語單字，這是英語語言的特性。英語假如沒有這種特性，狄克森先生絕不敢這麼肯定斷言，300個單字就可以講英語了。

　　只要您出門旅遊、在辦公室、私人理容、購物等場合，與人約時間，講定了某一天，現在要確定是當天的幾點鐘，您要說：「那一天幾點？」，英語怎麼說？

　　您在居家、公務的場合，與人商量某件事，對方提出一個辦法，您不表同意，您要說：「那樣不行！」或「那行不通。」，英語怎麼說？

　　答案不用遠到美國去找，需要的會話，本書都有，例如：

那一天幾點？ **What time of day?**

那不行！ **That won't do.**

您看，是不是很簡單。

可是，一般學校教英文，總是先教學生背單字，100分的測驗，單字每每佔了十到二十分的份量，把學生都考怕了，誤導了真正英語學習的方向，到頭來，英語能力總停留在：「讀文章靠半猜，開口一句也講不來」的境界。

本書是專為英語單字不多，但立志講一口純正英語的人士而編寫，每一單元都以最有趣的實境會話，使用最簡單的單字，來教您怎麼開口說英語。

您最有效的學習方法，是先閱讀每個對話，熟悉英美人士如何用最簡單的單字來組合成句子，表達自己的想法，跟聽線上MP3，學習標準英語腔調。

本書的對話，都是實境對話，從線上MP3中您可以聽出示範老師說話時的情緒，學到每句話的使用時機和正確說法。

最重要的是，您不須再學三年五載，才能開口說英語，就像每一本美國AA Bridgers公司，針對亞洲人士所設計的英語教材一樣，您從本書學到任何一句話，馬上就開口使用，與您交談的外國客戶、友人，會以為您在國外住過很久，英語才會這麼純正、流利，如此一來，您的信心就會徹底建立，英語也會說得越來越好。

前言 觀光旅遊、移民生活、留學遊學，
看這本就夠了 2

Chapter 1 搭飛機旅遊

Unit 1

預訂機位

Dialog 1

謝謝你打電話來美國航空公司。	Thank you for calling American Airlines.
有什麼事嗎？	How may I help you?
我想預訂一個四月二十日到東京的機位。	I'd like to make a reservation for one passenger on April 20 to Tokyo.
那一天幾點？	What time of day?
下午五點以前。	Before five p.m.
好的，小姐。	Okay, ma'am.

我們有一班下午三點二十七分的班機。	We have a flight at 3:27 p.m.
那班飛機可以。	That sounds great.

Dialog 2

好了，小姐。	Okay, ma'am.
在第二十四排我們有一個座位。	We have a seat on row 24.
那一排是在緊急出口處。	It's an emergency exit row.
不，那不行。	No, that won't do.
我是替我女兒預訂機位。	The reservation is for my daughter.
她才十一歲。	She is only 11 years old.
她要搭飛機到她姨媽家裡去住。	She's flying to her aunt's house to live.

好的，妳先把妳女兒的名字給我。	Okay, let me go ahead and get your daughter's name.
我可以把她換在第十九排。	I can put her on row 19 instead.
好的。她的名字是林瑪麗。	Good. Her name is Mary Lin.
她必須要帶著一個確認號碼。	She'll need to bring a confirmation number with her.
這個確認號碼是139-277。	The confirmation number is 139-277.
好的。謝謝妳的幫忙！	Okay. Thank you for your help!
再見。	Good-bye.

vocabulary

reservation [rɛzɚˈveʃən]		預訂
passenger [ˈpæsn̩dʒɚ]		乘客
emergency [ɪˈmɝdʒənsɪ]		緊急
exit [ˈɛgzɪt]		出口
row [ro]		排

ma'am [mæm]	（尊稱）女士
flight [flaɪt]	班機
seat	座位
instead [ɪn'stɛd]	而不
confirmation [ˌkɑnfə'meʃən]	確認

Unit 2

再確認機位

Dialog 1

謝謝你打電話來美國航空公司。	Thank you for calling American Airlines.
有什麼事嗎？	How may I help you?
我必須再確認我預定的機位。	I need to reconfirm a flight reservation.
你叫什麼名字？	Your name?

林南西。但是機位不是替我訂的。	Nancy Lin. But it's not for me.
是給我女兒，瑪莉。	It's for my daughter, Mary.
妳可以稍等一下嗎？	Could you please hold?
好的。	Yes.

Dialog 2

好的，我回來了。	Okay, I'm back.
訂位的是林瑪麗嗎？	Was that Mary Lin?
是的。	Yes.
我這裡顯示有一個林瑪麗預訂的機位，四月二十號飛往東，三點二十七分起飛。	I'm showing a reservation for Mary Lin on April 20 to Tokyo, departing at 3:27.
座位號碼幾號？	And what was the seat number?

是19E。	19 E.
那沒有錯。	That sounds just right.
謝謝你，再見。	Thank you, good-bye.

vocabulary

reconfirm [ˌrɪkənˈfɝm]	再確認
hold	稍等
back	回來
departing [dɪˈpɑrtɪŋ]	離開（depart 的現在分詞）

Unit 3

到機場

Dialog 1

下一位。	Next in line!

我要替我女兒報到登機。	Hi. I need to check in for my daughter.
她要前往東京。	She's going to Tokyo.
好的，是四點十九分的班機嗎？	Okay, was that the 4:19 flight?
不是，是三點二十七分起飛的那一班。	No, the one that departs at 3:27.
我們大約誤點十五分鐘。	We're running behind schedule by about 15 minutes.
登機時間大約在三點二十分開始。	Boarding will start probably about 3:20.
但是如果妳把確認號碼給我，我可以現在幫她登記，給妳登機證。	But if I could get the confirmation number, I can check her in now and give you a boarding pass.
謝謝你。	Thank you.
確認號碼在這兒，是139-277。	It's right here, 139-277.

Dialog 2

林瑪麗，飛往東京，座位號碼19E，對嗎？	Mary Lin, going to Tokyo, seat 19 E?
是的。	That's right.
登機證在這兒。	Here's the boarding pass.
那一位就是瑪麗嗎？	Is that Mary?
是的。	Yes.
祝妳一路順風！	Have a great flight!
來，瑪麗。	Come on, Mary.
我們就在這裡坐到妳上飛機的時間。	Let's sit over here until it's time for you to board.

vocabulary

line	排隊
depart [dɪˈpɑrt]	離開
schedule [ˈskɛdʒʊl]	日程安排
boarding [ˈbordɪŋ]	上飛機

probably [ˈprɑbəblɪ]	可能的
confirmation [ˌkɑnfɚˈmeʃən]	確認
pass	通行證
boarding pass	登機證
board [bord]	上（飛機、火車）

Unit 4
飛機上的飲食

Dialog 1

你好，先生。你晚餐要吃什麼？	Hi. What can I get for your dinner, sir?
你們有什麼？	What do you have?
我們可以讓你選火腿三明治、或是烤馬鈴薯。	We have a choice of a ham sandwich or a baked potato.
我要火腿三明治。	I'll have the ham sandwich.

你要喝什麼？	And what would you like to drink?
請給我一杯可樂。	I'll have a coke, please.

Dialog 2

哈囉，瑪莉。	Hello, Mary.
這趟飛行還好嗎？	How's your flight going?
好玩嗎？	Are you having fun?
還好。	It's okay.
我口渴了。	I'm thirsty.
我要一杯可樂。	I want a coke.
好的。	All right.
還有，你要三明治還是烤馬鈴薯？	And do you want the sandwich or the baked potato?
我想我要三明治。	I guess I want the sandwich.

好的，我馬上拿給你。	Okay, I'll have that right out.
如果你需要其它什麼東西，就告訴我。	Just let me know if you need anything else.
謝謝你。	Thanks.

vocabulary

choice
[tʃɔɪs]
選擇

baked
烤的

potato
[pəˈteto]
馬鈴薯

thirsty
口渴的

sandwich
三明治

MEMO

Chapter 2

在郵局

Unit 1

寄信

Dialog 1

下一位！	Next in line!
嗨，我要用快遞寄這一封信。	Hi. I need to send this letter by priority mail.
我們有一夜送達的『隔夜快遞』，價錢比較高。	We have higher rates for overnight delivery.
好，這一封信很重要。	Yes, this is very important.
好的。	All right.
讓我來秤一秤。	Let me weigh it.

好，那要三塊八毛二美金。	Okay, that will be $3.82.
在這兒。	Here you go.

數錢……

三塊……， 我想我有零錢，請稍等……	Three... I think I have the change, hold on...

Dialog 2

你找得到零錢嗎？	Can you find the change?
我相信應該找得到。	I believe so.
讓我看看。在這兒。	Let's see. **Here.**
好的。	All right.
我需要收據。	I need a receipt, please.
三塊八毛二，很好。	Three and eighty-two, very good.

收據在這兒。	There's your receipt.
希望你一整天都很愉快！	You have a nice day!
謝謝你，彼此彼此。	Thank you, you too.
再見。	Good-bye.

vocabulary

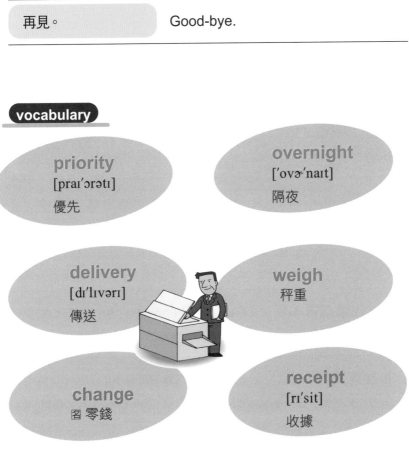

priority
[praɪˈɔrətɪ]
優先

overnight
[ˈovɚˈnaɪt]
隔夜

delivery
[dɪˈlɪvərɪ]
傳送

weigh
秤重

change
图 零錢

receipt
[rɪˈsit]
收據

寄包裹

Dialog 1

嗨，我需要一個可以裝得下這些東西的信。	Hi, I need a package that will hold these.
我相信我們的中型信 可以裝得下那些東西。	I believe our mid-size envelope will hold those things.
那種信封的內面墊有泡泡包裝紙嗎？	Does it have bubble wrap on the inside for padding?
有的。	Yes, it does.
好，我還得借一隻筆來填寫地址。	Okay, and I need a pen to fill out the address.
筆在這兒。你可以到那邊去寫，好讓我招呼下一位客人。	Here. You can fill it out over there while I wait on the next customer.

Dialog 2

我填完了。	I've finished.
很好。	Very good.
現在我來把它秤一下。	I'll just weigh that now.
這包裹要多久才會送到台灣？	How long will it take before the package arrives in Taiwan?
六至七天。	Six to seven days.
總共是十二塊五毛。	That's going to cost $12.50.
你收支票嗎？	Can I write a check?
有的，小姐。	Yes, ma'am.

vocabulary

package [ˈpækɪdʒ]	包裹
envelope [ˈɛnvəlop]	信封
hold	容納
bubble wrap	泡泡的包裝紙
padding [ˈpædɪŋ]	襯墊

fill out	填寫
wait on	服務
customer [ˈkʌstəmɚ]	客人

Unit 3
開郵政信箱

Dialog 1

有什麼事嗎？	How can I help you?
我想要開一個郵政信箱。	I'd like to get a post office box.
你準備用來收大件包裹嗎？	Are you expecting to receive large packages?
不會，只是商業信件。	No, just business letters.
一個小的郵政信箱六個月費用二十塊。	A small one costs $20 for six months.

那邊有你需要填寫的表格。	There are forms that you must fill out.
小郵政信箱滿好的。	The small one sounds good.
我應該在哪裡簽名？	Where do I sign?

Dialog 2

就是這張表格。	This is the form.
我需要你先填寫上半部。	I need you to fill out the top portion first.
我是不是該在下面這兒簽名？	Do I sign here at the bottom?
是的，先生。	Yes, sir.
所有的資料都填完之後，你就在這兒簽名。	Once all the information is completed, you sign here.
總共是二十元。	And that will be twenty dollars.
好的。	All right.

expecting [ɪksˈpɛktɪŋ]	預計（expect 的現在分詞）
receive [rɪˈsiv]	收到
business	生意
sign [saɪn]	簽名
top	上面
portion [ˈporʃən]	部分
bottom [ˈbɑtəm]	下面
information	資料

Unit 4

購買郵簡

Dialog 1

下一位。	Next.
哈囉，請問你要什麼？	Hello, how may I help you?

我需要買一些三十二分錢郵票，還有一些郵簡。	I need to buy some 32-cent stamps and some aerograms.
我們現有的三十二分郵票都是這些有自由女神像的。	All we have in the 32-cent stamps are these with the Statue of Liberty.
事實上，我滿喜歡的。	Actually, I like those.
是這樣嗎！你要多少張？	Really! How many do you need?
五十張。	Fifty.

Dialog 2

郵簡的樣子就是這樣。	This is what the aerogram looks like.
我想我大約需要五張郵簡。	I think I need about five of those.
哦，還有你能不能也讓我看看六十分錢的郵票？	Oh, and could I also look at the 60-cent stamps?

請等一下！	Just a moment.
我們現在有的就是這些。	Here is what we have right now.
你們有沒有天鵝圖案的郵票？	Do you have any of the swan stamps?
有的，我們有。	Yes, we do.
我要兩大張那種郵票。	I'll take two sheets of those also.

vocabulary

aerogram ['ɛrə,græm]	航空郵簡
stamp	郵票
statue ['stætʃʊ]	雕像
the Statue of Liberty	自由女神像（美國紐約）
actually ['æktʃʊəlɪ]	事實上
right now	現在
swan	天鵝
sheet [ʃit]	一張（紙）
a sheet of stamps	美國郵票一大張（有五十張郵票）

Chapter 3

到銀行

....

Unit 1

問如何開戶

Dialog 1

嗨，我要知道各種不同的支票帳戶和儲蓄帳戶，我應該跟誰談？	Hi, can I speak with someone about the different checking and savings accounts here?
好的，我可以幫你的忙。	Yes, I can help you.
請那邊坐。	Just have a seat right over there.
那些餅乾你可以自己取用。	Help yourself to any of those cookies.
好好噢！有餅乾！	Yum. Cookies!

言歸正傳。我是個學生。	Anyway. I'm a student.
我在想你們是不是有手續費較低的帳戶。	And I am wondering if you have any accounts with low service charges.
有，我們有。	Yes, we do.
如果你可以給我們看你現在的學生證，以證明你在學校註冊，我可以讓你開「學生支票戶」。	If you can prove your enrollment in school by showing a current student ID, I can hook you up with our Student Checking Account.
那種帳戶的條件是什麼？	What are the terms of that account?
只要你使用的是自動櫃員機，就不用每個月手續費。	There is no monthly service charge as long as you use ATM machines.
而且免費送你第一本支票。	And your first box of checks is free.

Dialog 2

那麼儲蓄存款帳戶呢？	What about savings accounts?
我們大部份儲蓄存款帳戶都要求很高的最低存款額。	Most of our savings accounts require a very high minimum balance.
但是有一種你可能辦得到。	But there is one that you might be able to manage.
你可以維持最少一塊錢的存款嗎？	Can you make a minimum $100 deposit?
可以。	Yes.
那好，開戶需要一美元。	Good. It's $100 to open.
而如果你的存款低於兩百五十塊，每個月要收很低的手續費三塊五。	And if your balance is below $250, there is a low monthly service fee of $3.50.

vocabulary

different 不同的

account [əˈkaʊnt]	帳戶
checking account	支票戶頭
savings account	儲蓄存款戶頭
cookies [ˈkʊkɪz]	餅乾（cookie 的複數）
service charge	手續費
prove	證明
enrollment [ɪnˈrolmənt]	入學
current [ˈkɝənt]	現時的；當前的
terms [tɝmz]	條件；條款
ATM machine	自動櫃員機
minimum [ˈmɪnɪməm]	最低限度
balance [ˈbæləns]	（在銀行的）結餘

Unit 2

開銀行帳戶

Dialog 1

哪一位是林約翰？	John Lin?

我就是。	That's me.
往這裡走，請坐在這一張桌子前面。	Right this way, just have a seat in front of this desk here.
請問你需要什麼服務？	What is it I can do for you?
我想要開一個儲蓄存款帳戶。	I want to open a savings account.
你要從目前的帳戶轉存嗎？	Will you be transferring funds from a current account?
不，我有一張八千塊的匯票，還有一些零錢。	No, I have this money order for $8,000 and some change.

Dialog 2

你要開『黃金儲蓄存款帳戶』嗎？	Do you want the Gold Savings account?
那種帳戶有哪些條件？	What are the options on that?

嗯，每天的存款額最少五千美元。	Well, it's a $5,000 minimum daily balance.
它的利息是最高的。	And it has the highest interest rate.
聽起來好像是最好的一種。	That sounds like the best one.
我的身分證和匯票在這兒。	Here's my ID and the money order.
好的，約翰。	Okay, John.
我先鍵入你的住址，然後開戶。	Let me type in your address and then open the account.
可能需要幾分鐘時間。	It might take a few minutes.
你可以在那張匯票上背書嗎？	Can I get you to endorse that money order?
好的，可以！	Yes, sure!

vocabulary

in front of　　　　　　　　　　在～之前

transferring ['trænsfɜ·ɪŋ]	轉帳
fund	存款
money order	匯票
change	零錢
option ['ɑpʃən]	供顧客選擇的條款
daily	每日的
interest rate	利息
ID	身分證件
endorse [ɪn'dɔrs]	背書

Unit 3

開儲蓄存款帳戶

Dialog 1

嗨,我先生和我想要開『共同存款帳戶』。	Hi, my husband and I would like to open a joint account.
好的,請往這邊走。	Okay, right this way.

我叫史蒂夫。您大名是……？	I'm Steve. And You?
我叫瑪麗。	I'm Mary.
這是我先生，約翰。	This is my husband, John.
您好，約翰。	Hi, John.
你們當中有哪位目前已有戶頭嗎？	Does either of you have a current account?
我們有一個『共同支票帳戶』。	We do have a joint checking account.
你需要帳號嗎？	Do you need the account number?
如果地址一樣的話，你把帳號給我，可以辦得快一點。	That would make it easier as long as the address remains the same.

Dialog 2

地址是一樣的。	The address is the same.

但是我們想開一個儲蓄存款帳戶，另外可能也要一個定期存款。	But we want a savings account and possibly a CD.
好的，我們先來開儲蓄存款帳戶。	Okay, let's do the savings account first.
最低存款額是一千美元。	There is a $1,000 minimum deposit.
一千五百元可以嗎？	How does $1,500 sound?
很好。	That sounds good to me.
是現金嗎？	Will that be cash?
不是，我這個人從不帶那麼多現金在身上。	No, I'm not one to carry around that much cash.
我們剛收到一張四千五百元的支票。	We just got a check for $4,500.
我們考慮放三千元在定期存款。	We were thinking of putting $3,000 in a CD.

另外一千五百元在儲蓄存款帳戶。	And $1,500 in savings.
好的，請在支票上背書，我會替你們把它分在兩個帳戶。	Okay, just endorse the check and I'll divide it up for you.
你們要兩年的定期存款嗎？	Did you want a two-year CD?

vocabulary

joint account	共同存款帳戶
remain [rɪˈmen]	保持不變
possibly	可能地
deposit	存款
cash	現金
CD	定期存款
check	支票
divide [dɪˈvaɪd]	分開

Unit 4

定期存款

Dialog 1

約翰，你看怎麼樣？	What do you think, John?
我認為最好放三千五百元在定存。	I think it would be better to put $3,500 in the CD.
我還以為我們已經決定要放三千元。	I thought we had decided on $3,000.
但是如果我們放三千五的話，你就不會買那麼多新鞋子！	But if we put $3,500 in, you won't buy as many new shoes!
約翰！我從來不買鞋子的。	John! I never buy shoes.
我現在所有的鞋子都是破的，全都兩年舊了。	All of mine are worn and two years old.

你買的鞋子都是一雙兩百美元的。	Your shoes cost $200 a pair.
我是情非得已，不得不這樣。	I can't help it.
我需要一雙好的鞋子，可以上班一整天穿！	I need good shoes to be on my feet all day at work!

Dialog 2

放三千塊在兩年的定期存款。	Put $3,000 in a two-year CD.
先別聽她的。	Don't listen to her yet.
我們還沒有達成協議。	We haven't agreed.
瑪麗，妳難道不認為我們應該至少再多放五百元在定期存款？	Mary, don't you think we should at least put $500 more in the CD?
那可以有更多的利息。	It would earn that much more interest.

好吧，如果你堅持的話。	All right, if you insist.

vocabulary

decided [dɪˈsaɪdɪd]	決定（decide 的過去分詞）
worn	破舊的（wear 的過去分詞）
agreed	已經同意（agree 的過去分詞）
at least	至少
earn [ɝn]	賺
insist [ɪnˈsɪst]	堅持己見

Unit 5

買旅行支票

Dialog 1

哈囉，先生。	Hello, sir.
您今天需要什麼嗎？	What can I do for you today?

嗨，我要到國外去旅行。	Hi. I'm traveling out of the country.
我需要買一些旅行支票。	And I need to buy some traveler's checks.
美國運通公司的旅行支票可以嗎？	Will American Express traveler's checks be all right?
可以。請你快點，我的飛機再兩小時就要起飛。	Yes. Please hurry, my flight leaves in two hours.
你需要幾張旅行支票？	How many traveler checks do you want?
我需要五千塊旅行支票。	I'll need five thousand dollars' worth.

Dialog 2

下一位。	Next in line, please.
哈囉，瑪麗，我不知道你今天有上班。	Hello, Mary, I didn't know you are working today.
嗨，約翰。你好。	Hi, John. Good to see you.

你需要什麼？	What can I do for you?
我需要兩千元的旅行支票。	I need two thousand dollars in traveler's checks, please.
照辦！	Sure thing.
你知道旅行支票要繳百分之一的手續費嗎？	Do you know there's a one percent fee for traveler's checks?
我知道，沒有關係。	Yes, that's fine with me.

vocabulary

traveling
['trævḷɪŋ]
（ travel的現在分詞 ）

country
國家

traveler's check
旅行支票

worth
價值

line
排隊

43

MEMO

Chapter 4 電話英語

MP3-05

Unit 1

約翰在嗎？

Dialog 1

瑪麗接電話……

哈囉。	Hello.
嗨，請問你是誰？	Hi. Who am I speaking with?
我是瑪麗。	This is Mary.
你是誰？	Who are you?
我的名字是約翰。	My name's John.
珍在嗎？	Is Jane there?
不，她不在。	No, she's not.

45

你要留話給她嗎？	May I take a message?
不，沒關係。	No, that's all right.
我以後再打給她。	I'll call her back later.

Dialog 2

瑪麗接電話……

我是瑪麗。	Mary speaking.
嗨，瑪麗。	Hi, Mary.
你好嗎？	How are you doing?
約翰！我好久沒有你的消息了！	John! I haven't heard from you in ages!
是啊。我最近一直很忙，所以沒時間打電話給任何人。	Yeah. I've been so busy lately. I haven't had time to call anybody.
你現在在家嗎？	Are you at home right now?
不，我現在在公司。	No, I'm in the office right now.

vocabulary

message ['mɛsɪdʒ]		留言
later		稍後
heard [hɝd]	聽到 （hear的過去分詞）	
lately		最近的
office		辦公室

Unit 2

辦公室電話英語

Dialog 1

這裡是新娘花卉佈置公司。	Bridal Blooms and Arrangements.
我是瑪麗。	Mary speaking.
你需要什麼嗎？	How may I help you?

嗨，我不知道你們能不能建議一下，我的婚禮該怎麼佈置花卉。	Hi, I was wondering if you could suggest some flower arrangements for my wedding.
可以，你要不要過來聽取諮詢？	Sure, would you like to come in for a consultation?
諮詢是免費的嗎？	Is the consultation free?
事實上，諮詢費是五十美元，而且是不能退的。	Actually, there's a fifty dollar, non-refundable consultation fee.
很抱歉，我負擔不起。	I'm sorry, but I can't afford that.

Dialog 2

KPG會計公司，我是瑪麗。	KPG Accounting, Mary speaking.
有什麼事嗎？	How can I help you?
我是李約翰。	This is John Lee speaking.
史蒂夫在嗎？	Is Steve in?

很抱歉，史蒂夫正在開一個視訊會議。	I'm sorry but Steve is in a video conference right now.
你要留話給他嗎？	Can I take a message?
請告訴他，他的建議我已經考慮過了。	Tell him I've considered his proposal.
我認為公司合併是一個很明智的決定。	And I think the merger is a wise decision.
很好，先生。	Very well, sir.
就這些嗎？	Is that all?
請告訴他，在他方便的時間，我想跟他見面談一些生意機會。	Tell him I'd like to meet with him about some business opportunities at his next convenience.

vocabulary

wondering [ˈwʌndərɪŋ]	想知道（wonder 的現在分詞）	
suggest		建議
arrangement [əˈrendʒmənt]		安排

wedding	婚禮
consultation [ˌkɑnsḷˈteʃən]	諮詢
refundable	可退費的
non-refundable	不退費的
fee	費用
afford [əˈfɔrd]	負擔得起
video	影像的
conference	會議
merger [ˈmɝdʒɚ]	公司合併
decision	決定
opportunities [ˌɑpɚˈtjunətɪz]	機會（opportunity 的複數）
convenience [kənˈvinjəns]	方便

Unit 3

旅館電話

Dialog 1

假日旅館。	Holiday Inn.
我是瑪麗。	This is Mary.

哈囉。	Hello.
我想知道有沒有一位叫林約翰的，在你們那兒投宿。	I was wondering if there is a John Lin registered there.
請等一下，讓我查查登記簿。	One moment please while I check the directory.
我會在電話上等著。	I'll hold.

查完登記簿……

先生，很對不起，沒有噢。	No, sir, I'm sorry.
沒有人用那個名字在這裡登記投宿。	There's no one by that name registered here.
嗯，謝謝你花時間幫我找。	Well, thank you for your time.

Dialog 2

希爾頓大飯店。	Hilton Hotel.

你需要什麼嗎？	What can we do for you?
嗨，我六月六號需要在紐約訂一間房間。	Hi, I need to make a reservation for June 6 in New York.
在紐約我們有兩家希爾頓飯店。	We have two Hiltons in New York.
你較喜歡哪一家？	Which would you prefer?
哪一家較靠近海灘我就要那一家。	Whichever is closer to the beach.
好的，你要兩張單人床，還是一張中號的床？	OK, would you prefer two single beds or one queen size bed?
我單獨旅行。	I'm traveling alone.
所以我只需要一張床。	So I'll only be needing one bed.

vocabulary

registered [ˈrɛdʒɪstɚd]	登記住宿（register的過去式）	
moment [ˈmomənt]		片刻

directory [dəˈrɛktərɪ]	登記簿；電話簿
line	電話線
prefer [prɪˈfɝ]	較喜歡
beach	海灘
alone	單獨的

Unit 4

查號台

Dialog 1

要哪一個城市？	What city, please?
這裡是查號台嗎？	Is this Directory assistance?
是的。	Yes, it is.
你想查哪一個城市？	What city are you calling for, please?
嗯，我想是在達拉斯。	Well, I think it's in Dallas.

是什麼名字？	What's the name?
我想它是叫做ABC公司。	I think it's called ABC Company.

Dialog 2

這裡是查號台。	Directory assistance.
你要打哪一個城市？	What city are you calling for?
洛杉磯。	It's in Los Angeles.
好的。	OK.
你需要誰的號碼？	Whose number do you need?
名字是林瑪麗。	The name is Mary Lin.
請等一下。	One moment, please.
號碼是5-5-5-4-5-6-7。	The number is 5-5-5-4-5-6-7.
非常謝謝。	Thank you very much.

你可以幫我接通嗎？	Could you please connect me?

vocabulary

directory
電話號碼簿

assistance
[əˈsɪstəns]
幫助

place
地方

number
電話號碼

connect
[kəˈnɛkt]
接通（電話）

MEMO

Chapter 5

到旅館

Unit 1

旅館訂房間

Dialog 1

哈囉，這裡是希爾頓飯店。	Hello, this is the Hilton Hotel.
你需要什麼嗎？	How can I help you?
嗨，我要訂一間雙人房，下禮拜五和禮拜六。	Hi, I need to make a reservation for two for Friday and Saturday of next week.
你要指定吸煙或不吸煙的房間嗎？	Will you be requiring a smoking or non-smoking room?
我比較想要不吸煙的房間。	I would prefer non-smoking.

Chapter 5

你需要兩張床還是一張床？	Will you need two beds or one?
我是替我自己和我太太訂房間。	The reservation's for me and my wife.
所以我們只要一張床。	So we'll only be requiring one bed.

Dialog 2

這裡是假日旅館。	Holiday Inn.
我是約翰，有什麼事嗎？	John speaking, how may I help you?
嗨，我可以訂一個房間給兩個大人三個小孩嗎？	Hi, can I reserve a room for two adults and three children?
通常我們不允許五個人住一個房間。	We normally don't allow five people in one room.
我的小孩還很小。	My children are young.

我要他們跟我同住一個房間，好照顧他們。	And I need them to be in the same room so I can keep an eye on them.
很好。	Very well.
我們可以在我們的一間雙人房裡多擺一張床。	We can put an extra bed into one of our rooms with two beds.
訂的是哪一天晚上？	What night will this be for?
是六月的第一個週末，我們需要這個房間。	I will need the room for the first weekend in June.

vocabulary

requiring [rɪˈkwaɪrɪŋ]	要求（require 的現在分詞）
smoking	抽煙的
reserve [rɪˈzɝv]	預定
adult	大人
normally	通常
keep an eye on ~	看顧～
extra [ˈɛkstrə]	多餘的

旅館的服務生

Dialog 1

先生，要我幫你拿行李嗎？	May I carry your bags for you, sir?
事實上，我完全自己可以拿。	Actually, I am quite capable of carrying my own bags.
先生，我知道。	Very well, sir.
但是我是個服務生，所以我不介意幫你拿。	But I am the porter, so I don't mind.
哦，對不起。	Oh, I'm sorry.
我不知道那是你的工作。	I didn't realize this was your job.
沒有關係的。	It's quite all right.

讓我來幫你拿那些吧。	Let me get those for you.
非常謝謝你。	Thank you very much.
我很感謝你的幫忙。	I appreciate the help.

Dialog 2

謝謝你幫我拿行李。	Thank you for carrying my bags.
小姐，不用客氣。	No problem, ma'am.
這是我份內的事。	Just doing my job!
這是小費，給你。	Here is your tip.
每一分錢都你都得之無愧。	You deserve every penny of it.
謝謝你。	Thank you.
謝謝你這麼慷慨大方。	I appreciate your generosity.

carry [ˈkærɪ]	拿
bags	行李；袋子（bag的複數）
capable [ˈkæpəbl̩]	有能力的
porter [ˈportɚ]	（車站、飯店）提行李員
mind	介意
realize	知道
appreciate [əˈprɪʃɪˌet]	感激
tip	小費
deserve [dɪˈzɝv]	應得的
generosity [ˌdʒɛnəˈrɑsətɪ]	慷慨

Unit 3
旅館的服務台

Dialog 1

嗨，有誰可以過來幫我嗎？	Hey, could someone help me over here?

先生，我馬上過來。	I'll be with you in a moment, sir.
我正在講電話。	I'm on the phone.
我沒有時間等。	I don't have time to wait.
你可以告訴我『舊金山牛排館』在哪裡？	Could you please tell me where the San Francisco Steak House is?
先生，我正在講電話。	Sir, I'm on the phone.
請你等一下，我會來幫你的。	If you would only wait a moment I could help you.
小姐，我很不欣賞你的態度。	I do not appreciate your attitude, young lady.
先生，很抱歉。	I apologize, sir.
但是，我正在處理一通很重要的電話。	But I'm trying to take care of a very important call.

Dialog 2

小姐，對不起。	Excuse me, ma'am.

這裡是服務台嗎？	Is this the information desk?
是啊。	Yes, it is.
有什麼事嗎？	What can I do for you?
不知道你們有沒有本地觀光勝地的小手冊。	I was wondering if you had any brochures for local tourist attractions.
有的。	Certainly.
我們本地有許多不同的觀光勝地。	We have a wide array of attractions in the area.
你心中有特別中意，想參觀的嗎？	What did you have in mind?
我太太想要看有歷史性的紀念碑。	My wife wants to see historical monuments.
我們這附近有很多歷史性的紀念碑。	We have many of those in the area.
這裡是一些小冊子。	Here are some brochures.

attitude
['ætɪtjud]
態度

apologize
[ə'palədʒaɪz]
道歉

information desk
服務台

brochure
[bro'ʃjʊr]
小冊子

local
當地的

tourist
旅客

attraction
[ə'trækʃən]
具有吸引力的事物

tourist attractions
觀光勝地

certainly
['sɝtn̩lɪ]
當然

area
地區

array
排列

monument
['manjəmənt]
紀念碑；紀念塔

historical
[hɪs'tɔrɪkl̩]
歷史的

登記住宿

Dialog 1

嗨，我要登記住宿。	Hi. I'm here to check in.
先生，你是什麼大名？	What's your name, sir?
我的名字是林約翰。	My name's John Lin.
但是房間可能是用我太太的名字預訂的。	But the reservation's probably under my wife's name.
那麼，你太太的大名是…？	Well then, what is your wife's name?
她的名字是林瑪麗。	Her name is Mary Lin.
有了，我們為你們訂了二一六號房。	Yes, we have you in room 216.

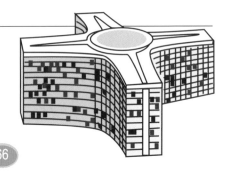

Dialog 2

哈囉，先生。你需要什麼幫忙嗎？	Hello, sir. Can I help you with something?
是的，你可以幫我。	Yes, you can help me.
你可以給我一間房間。	You can give me a room.
我已經開了一整天的車，已經快睡著了。	I've been driving all day and can hardly stay awake.
先生，你有預訂房間嗎？	Do you have a reservation, sir?
我當然有預訂房間！	Of course I have a reservation!
我知道在冬天這間旅館很快就客滿。	I know how quickly this hotel fills up in the winter.
是啊，現在是旺季。	Yes, it is very busy right now.
你說你的大名是…？	What did you say your name was?
哦，是的，抱歉。	Oh, yes. I'm sorry.

| 我的名字是林約翰。 | My name is John Lin. |

Unit 5

客房服務

Dialog 1

knock, knock 敲門聲⋯⋯

| 我是客房服務。 | Room service! |

| 我馬上就過來開門。 | I'll be there in a moment. |

| 先生，慢慢來，沒關係。 | Take your time, sir. |

很抱歉，這麼久才來開門。	I'm sorry it took me so long to reach the door.
這是我點的火腿三明治嗎？	Is this the ham sandwich I ordered?
是的，先生。還要其它什麼東西嗎？	Yes, sir. Will there be anything else?
不需要，非常謝謝你。	No, thank you very much.
我只是有一點餓。	I'm just a little bit hungry.

Dialog 2

knock, knock 敲門聲……

林先生，客房服務。	Room service, Mr. Lin.
哈囉。你是否拿新毛巾來給我？	Hello. Are you here to bring me fresh towels?
是的，我還多帶了一些肥皂和洗髮精給你。	Yes, I also have more soap and shampoo for you.

非常謝謝你。	Thank you so much.
我肥皂快要用完了。	I was almost out of soap.
這種事常常發生的。	That happens quite frequently.
大家很快就把肥皂用完。	People go through soap very quickly.
我想是吧。	I suppose so.
你想我是不是可以再多要一塊肥皂？	Do you think I might be able to have an extra bar of soap?

vocabulary

knock [nɑk]		敲門聲
service		服務
reach [ritʃ]		到達
order		點（菜）
hungry		飢餓的
shampoo [ʃæmˈpu]		洗髮精
fresh [frɛʃ]		新的
towel		毛巾
frequently [ˈfrikwəntlɪ]		經常的
suppose		假定

Unit 6

退房

Dialog 1

這是房間鑰匙。	Here is the room key.
林先生，您住得還愉快嗎？	Did you enjoy your stay here, Mr. Lin?
哦，很好，一切都很好。	Oh yes, it was lovely.
服務生很友善。	The porters were friendly.
客房服務也很棒。	And the room service was excellent.
那是我們最喜歡聽到的。	That's what we like to hear.

下次我再到本地，還會來你們這兒住。	I'm certainly coming back here next time I'm in town.
我們期待很快再見到你。	We look forward to seeing you again soon.

Dialog 2

林先生，你要退房嗎？	Are you checking out, Mr. Lin?
是我，我要趕快回台南去，因為我的太太快要生產了。	Yes, I must hurry back to Tainan because my wife is in labor.
恭喜你！	Congratulations!
你一定很興奮。	You must be very excited.
是的，可否請你快一點？	Yes, could you please hurry?
我必須馬上離開。	I must leave right away.
很抱歉。	I'm sorry.
這是你的收據。	Here's your receipt.

謝謝你選擇住『假日旅館』。	Thank you for choosing the Holiday Inn.
不客氣。	You're welcome.
外面有計程車嗎？	Are there cabs outside?

vocabulary

enjoy	喜歡
excellent [ˈɛksələnt]	很棒
friendly	友善的
look forward to V-ing	期待
check out	退房
in labor	正要生產
congratulations [kən͵grætʃəˈleʃənz]	恭喜
excited [ɪkˈsaɪtɪd]	興奮
hurry [ˈhɝɪ]	匆忙
receipt [rɪˈsɪt]	收據
cab	計程車

MEMO

Chapter 6 談音樂

Unit 1

喜歡什麼音樂？

Dialog 1

哦，我好喜歡麥可傑克森的這一首新歌！	Oh, I just love this new song by Michael Jackson!
我不喜歡麥可傑克森。	I don't like Michael Jackson.
我較喜歡美國鄉村音樂。	I like country music much more.
你瘋了嗎？	Are you crazy?!
沒有一個鄉村歌手比得上麥可傑克森。	There isn't a single country singer who's as good as Michael Jackson.

格司布魯克斯比麥可傑克森好多了。	Garth Brooks is much better than Michael Jackson.
你不知道什麼是好的音樂。	You don't know what good music is.
鄉村音樂好乏味。	Country music is too boring.
麥可傑克森是個瘟三。	Michael Jackson is a wimp.
如果你喜歡他，那你也是一個瘟三。	And if you like him, you're a wimp, too.

Dialog 2

你有沒有聽過『畢斯地男孩』所推出的新歌？	Have you heard that new song by the Beastie Boys?
你怎麼會聽饒舌歌呢？	Why do you listen to rap?
那跟你很喜歡的重金屬音樂並沒有什麼不同啊。	It's not much different from that heavy metal music you like so much.

重金屬音樂跟饒舌歌大大的不同。	Heavy metal music is a lot different from rap music.
你可以隨著重金屬音樂跳舞。	You can dance to heavy metal.
嘿，你也可以隨著饒舌歌跳舞啊！	Hey, you can dance to rap music!
我沒辦法隨著饒舌歌跳舞。	I can't dance to it.
我知道你也沒辦法，因為我看你試過。	And I know you can't either because I've seen you try.

vocabulary
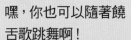

country music	鄉村歌曲
crazy ['krezɪ]	瘋狂的
singer	歌星
wimp [wɪmp]	（俗語）瘟三
rap	饒舌歌
metal ['mɛtl̩]	金屬

買CD

Dialog 1

在我買這張『瑪麗卡爾莉』的CD之前，我可不可以先試聽？	Can I listen to this Mary Carey CD before I buy it?
不行，很抱歉。	No, I'm sorry.
我們不能讓我們的顧客先試聽。	We don't allow our customers to do that.
那我怎麼知道它好不好呢？	How will I know if it's any good?
噢，我自己聽過那張CD，我很喜歡它。	Well, I've heard that CD and I liked it a lot.
就因為你喜歡它，不代表我也會喜歡。	Just because you liked it doesn't mean I will.
我對音樂的素養是很高的。	I usually have very good taste in music.

Dialog 2

你們有沒有『星際大戰』的電影原聲帶CD？	Do you have the "Star Wars" sound track on CD?
有的，在店裡的後面。	Yes, it's in the back of the store.
你要我拿一張給你嗎？	Do you want me to get it for you?
就請你幫我拿一張吧。	Would you please?
我馬上回來。	I'll be right back.
好了，在這裡。	OK, here you go.
多少錢？	How much does it cost?
是八塊九毛九，稅外加。	It's eight ninety-nine plus tax.
那是打折的價錢。	That's a sale price.

allow
允許

customer
顧客

mean
[min]
意味著；即是

taste
[test]
素養；品味

sound track
電影原聲帶

back
後面

tax
稅

Chapter 7

聽收音機

Unit 1

聽哪一個電台？

Dialog 1

我們可不可以換一個電台？	Can we please change the radio station?
你想聽哪個電台？	What station do you like?
94.5頻道有很好的音樂。	94.5 has pretty good music.
他們所播放的都是最新的。	Everything they play is brand new.
是沒錯，但是他們總是一再播放同一首歌。	Yeah, but they play the same songs over and over again.

那就選你要聽的電台好了。	Well, choose whatever station you want.
總之就是換個電台。	Just change the station.
好啦，我把它轉到頻道94.5。	Okay, I'll put it on 94.5.
但是只轉過去一會兒。	But just for a little while.

Dialog 2

把收音機調到頻道102.9。	Put the radio on 102.9.
他們正在進行一場比賽，我們可能贏得一千塊。	They're having a contest right now and we can win one thousand dollars.
每家電台現在都有比賽。	Every radio station is having a contest.
沒錯，但是一千塊可是一大筆錢噢。	Yeah, but a thousand dollars is a lot of money.

頻道92.5有個比賽，你可以贏兩萬塊。	92.5 has a contest where you can win twenty thousand dollars.
沒有人贏過那個比賽。	Nobody ever wins that contest.
你必須不斷聽著那個電台，才有贏的機會。	You would have to listen to that station all the time to even have a chance of winning.
我們還是選音樂最好聽的電台。	Let's just pick the station with the best music.
那家新頻道93.3怎麼樣？	How about that new one, 93.3?

vocabulary

change	換（收音機頻道）
radio	收音機
station ['steʃən]	電台
pretty ['prɪtɪ]	相當的
pretty good	相當好
choose	選擇
contest ['kɑntɛst]	比賽
win	贏

談論電台節目

Dialog 1

這個電台廣告太多了。	This station has too many commercials.
每一個電台廣告都很多。	Every station has too many commercials.
你何不轉到一個沒有廣告的電台？	Why don't you change the station to one where they aren't playing commercials?
每一個電台都有廣告。	Every station plays commercials.
不，我的意思是說，轉到一家現在沒在廣告的電台。	No, I mean change to a station that's not playing commercials right now.
但是，我喜歡這一個廣告。	But I like this commercial.

我喜歡頻道102.1這個叫做『連三投星期四』的節目。	I love triple-shot Thursday on 102.1.
『連三投星期四』是什麼節目？	What's triple-shot Thursday?
我從來不聽頻道102.1。	I never listen to 102.1.
哦，就是那個連續播放三首同一歌手歌的電台。	Oh, that's where they play three songs by the same artist back to back.
你的意思是說例如連續播放三首『U2樂團』不同的歌？	You mean like three different U2 songs all in a row?
是啊，那不是很好嗎？！	Yeah, isn't that cool?!
我猜是不錯。	I guess that's cool.

Chapter 7

除非你不喜歡某個樂團，因為那樣的話，你必須連聽三首爛歌。

Unless you don't like the band, in which case you have to listen to three bad songs in a row.

commercial
[kəˈmɝʃəl]
廣告；商業的

triple
[ˈtrɪpl̩]
三倍的

artist
藝術家

back to back
連續

in a row
連續

band
樂團

Chapter 8

看電視、報紙

Unit 1

選電視台

Dialog 1

電視遙控器在誰那兒？	Who has the remote control?
在我這兒。	I do.
怎麼了，你要我換個電視台嗎？	Why, do you want me to change the channel?
是的，請你換個台。	Yes, please.
我受不了看第三台。	I can't stand watching Channel 3.
我認為他們的節目很好。	I think they have pretty good programs.

但是，如果你要換也可以。	But I'll change it if you want.
轉到MTV。	Put it on MTV.
哦，我最討厭MTV。	Oh, I hate MTV.
我寧願聽收音機。	I'd rather just listen to the radio.

Dialog 2

約翰，我們應該看哪一個電台？	What channel should we watch, John?
哦，隨便都行。	Oh, I don't care.
我們何不把它轉到電影頻道？	Why don't we put it on movie channel?
好啊，他們通常播很好的電影。	Yeah, they usually have pretty good movies.
如果電影頻道沒什麼好看的，我們可以看看迪士尼頻道。	If there's nothing on movie channel, we can check out Disney's.

| 好奧妙喔，有這麼多頻道可供選擇。 | It's amazing how many channels you can choose. |
| 是啊，有時候實在很難決定要看什麼。 | Yeah, sometimes it's hard to decide what to watch. |

vocabulary

remote [rɪˈmot]
遙遠的

control
控制

remote control
遙控器

channel [ˈtʃænl]
電視頻道

video [ˈvɪdɪo]
影像；電視

program [ˈprogræm]
節目

stand
忍受

care
在乎

amazing [əˈmezɪŋ]
令人驚奇的

Unit 2

談電視節目

Dialog 1

這個節目很乏味。	This show is boring.
換個頻道。	Change the channel.
大腦手術的節目怎麼會乏味？	What's so boring about brain surgery?
我從來沒在電視上看過這一類的手術。	I've never seen this type of operation on TV.
我們何不看『急診室裡的春天』？	Why don't we watch "ER"?
教學節目有趣多了。	The learning channel is much more interesting.
它們總演些很吸引人的東西。	There's always something fascinating on.

我們上一回看到的是關於猴子怎樣生小猴。	The last show we watched was about how monkeys give birth.
拜託你換個頻道好嗎。	Please change the channel.
等這個節目結束之後,我就會換頻道。	I'll change the channel after the show's over.
我要看看這個傢伙完大腦手術後,反應怎樣。	I want to see how this guy acts after the brain surgery.

Dialog 2

哦,不好了!	Oh no!
我快錯過『X檔案』這個節目了。	I'm missing the X-Files.
約翰!換頻道!	John! Change the channel!
哎呀,我很高興你還記得。	Oh man, I'm glad you remembered.

我可喜歡那個節目了。	I love that show.
是啊，上一集裡莫德發現他媽媽被外星人綁架。	Yeah, the last episode Molder found out that his mom was kidnapped by aliens.
這個節目不僅僅是情節好看。	It's not just the plot that makes the show interesting, **though**.
我喜歡它的背景音樂和奇特的取景角度。	I like the music and the strange camera angles.
我知道你的意思。	I know what you mean.
看這個節目，就好像看電影一樣。	It's like watching a movie.

vocabulary

brain	大腦
surgery [ˈsɝdʒərɪ]	手術
operation [ˌɑpəˈreʃən]	手術
interesting	有趣的
fascinating [ˈfæsn̩ˌetɪŋ]	吸引人的
give birth	生

missing	錯過（miss 的現在分詞）
remember	記得
episode ['ɛpə,sod]	（電視劇集）一集
kidnapped ['kɪdnæpt]	被綁架（kidnap 的過去分詞）
plot	劇情
alien ['elɪən]	外星人
camera ['kæmərə]	攝影機；相機
angle ['æŋgl̩]	角度

Unit 3

早餐讀報

Dialog 1

夫婦早餐…

那，約翰，有什麼新聞嗎？	So, John, what's happening in the world?
嗯。	Mmmph.

『華爾街日報』上有沒有什麼有趣的事發生？	Is there anything interesting happening on Wall Street?
啊？	Huh?
我想你訓練自己哼哼哈哈，以便聽起來好像是在回答。	I think you train yourself to make noises so you'll sound like you're responding.
而仍然不理我。	But you can still somehow ignore me.
嗯哼。	Uh huh.

Dialog 2

這篇文章寫的是有關『遊騎兵隊』。	This article is about the Rangers.
是曲棍球的『遊騎兵隊』，還是棒球的？	The hockey team or the baseball team?
你提曲棍球隊是什麼意思？	What do you mean the hockey team?

我對在紐約的球隊沒興趣，我的意思是說除非他們輸球！	I'm not interested in New York teams...,that is, except for when they lose!
那說的是哪一隊？	So which is it?
是有關一支叫做『遊騎兵隊』的德州棒球隊，打敗一支叫做『洋基隊』的紐約棒球隊。	It's about a Texas baseball team called the Rangers beating a New York baseball team called the Yankees.
加油，『遊騎兵隊』！。	Go, Rangers!

vocabulary

world	世界
train [tren]	訓練
noise	噪音
responding [rɪsˈpandɪŋ]	反應（respond 的現在分詞）
ignore [ɪgˈnor]	不理睬
article [ˈartɪkl̩]	文章；報導
hockey [ˈhakɪ]	曲棍球
except	除了～之外
beating [ˈbitɪŋ]	打敗（beat 的現在分詞）

雜貨店買報紙

Dialog 1

媽，我可以買這份報紙嗎？	Mom, can I have this newspaper?
它說有一個像外星人的小孩子，跟一位脫口秀的主持人住在一起。	It says that there is an alien-like child living with a talk show host.
那不是報紙。	That's not a newspaper.
那是垃圾小型八卦報紙！	That's a trashy tabloid!
你怎麼不看『華爾街日報』？	Why don't you read about Wall Street?
我只有九歲耶！	I'm only nine!
我可以買這一個嗎？	Can I have this one?

那也是垃圾小型八卦報紙。	That is also a trashy tabloid.
它跟垃圾一樣差。	It's no better than garbage.
它看起來不像我會扔掉的東西。	It doesn't look like something I would throw away.
但它看起來就像我絕不會買的東西。	But it looks like something I would never buy.
你可以唸你的教科書去。	You can read your textbooks.

Dialog 2

哇。我不知道牧師也會坐牢。	Wow. I didn't even know priests could go to jail.
牧師也得受法律管轄。	They're not above the law.
怎麼了？發生什麼事了嗎？	Why? What happened?
有人在告牧師。	Someone's suing a priest.

喔，還有一個恐怖份子正要在紐約一棟辦公大樓放炸彈時，被抓到了。	Oh, and a terrorist was caught planting a bomb in an office building in New York.
恐怖份子通常把目標放在各州和國家的首都，不是嗎？	Terrorists usually go for those state and national capitals, don't they?
我不知道。	I don't know.
我又不是恐怖份子。	I'm not a terrorist.
你都不看報紙嗎？	Don't you read the paper?

98

tabloid
['tæblɔɪd]
小型八卦報紙

garbage
['gɑrbɪdʒ]
垃圾

textbook
['tɛkst,bʊk]
教科書

priest
[prist]
牧師

jail
獄

suing
['suɪŋ]
控告（sue的現在分詞）

bomb
[bɑm]
炸彈

terrorist
['tɛrərɪst]
恐怖份子

capital
['kæpɪtl̩]
首都

Chapter 8

MEMO

Chapter 9

娛樂和教育

....

Unit 1

在博物館

Dialog 1

瑪麗，妳以前到過這裡嗎？	Have you ever been here before, Mary?
沒有，這博物館好可愛。	No, the museum is so lovely.
謝謝你帶我來。	Thank you for bringing me.
哦，沒什麼。	Oh, no problem.
我一個月至少來一次。	I come here at least once a month.
他們的展覽經常更換。	The exhibits are constantly changing.

這裡不是應該有恐龍的展示嗎？	Isn't there supposed to be a dinosaur exhibit around here?
有，在西廂。	Yes, it's in the west wing.
跟我來。	Follow me.
我們到那邊去。	We'll go there.
我喜歡恐龍。	I love dinosaurs.
牠們又巨大又強壯。	They're so big and powerful.

Dialog 2

我記得小時候來過這兒，被那些大恐龍嚇壞了。	I remember coming here when I was a child and being scared by all the huge dinosaurs.
嗯，如果你不想看的話，我們可以避過恐龍不看。	Well, we can avoid the dinosaurs if you want.
不會的，沒關係。	No, that's all right.
我已經不再害怕了。	I'm not afraid anymore.

現在我覺得牠們很迷人。	I think they're fascinating now.
牠們是很迷人。	They are.
牠們也不能傷害你，除非是骨頭掉下來壓扁你。	They can't hurt you anyway...unless the bones were to fall over and crush you.
瑪麗，不要嚇我。	Mary, stop trying to scare me.
我聽說有一對情侶在看恐龍。	I heard about this one couple staring at a dinosaur.
結果恐龍的頭掉下來。	And its head just fell off.
他們兩個都被壓死。	They were both killed.

vocabulary

museum [mjuˈzɪəm]	博物館
lovely	很吸引人
exhibit [ɪgˈzɪbɪt]	展覽
constantly [ˈkɑnstəntlɪ]	不斷地
dinosaur [ˈdaɪnəˌsɔr]	恐龍
wing [wɪŋ]	廂房

powerful	強大的
scared [skɛrd]	害怕的（scare的過去分詞）
fascinating [ˈfæsn̩ˌetɪŋ]	迷人的
huge	巨大的
avoid	避開
crush [krʌʃ]	壓壞
scare	害怕

Unit 2

在畫廊

Dialog 1

你認為這一幅圖畫，應該是代表什麼？	What do you think this picture is supposed to represent?
嗯，有一碗水果，所以我認為它是代表食物。	Well, it's a bowl of fruit, so I suppose it represents food.

不，我是說它更深一層的意義？	No, I mean, what is the deeper meaning?
有一個橘子，一個蘋果，還有一個梨子。	There's an orange, an apple, and a pear.
我想這幅圖是告訴我們水果是生活中不可缺的。	I think it shows us how fruit is necessary to life.
嘿，那是很有趣的分析。	Hey, that's a very interesting analysis.
我喜歡。	I like that.
真的嗎？	Really?
我只是在開玩笑。	I was just making a joke.
但是如果你喜歡的話，我也喜歡。	But if you like it, I like it.

Dialog 2

這一張應該是畢卡索的最後的作品之一。	This is supposed to be one of Picasso's last works.

我不太喜歡它。	I don't really like it.
你不喜歡是什麼意思？	What do you mean you don't like it?
是畢卡索耶。	It's a Picasso.
每個人都喜歡畢卡索的！	Everybody likes Picasso!
我就不喜歡畢卡索，所以並不是每個人都喜歡畢卡索。	I don't like Picasso; therefore, not everybody likes Picasso.
我認為其實你不懂欣賞他的用色。	I don't think you can truly appreciate his use of colors.
我所知道的是，他的畫很醜，我不喜歡。	All I know is, his pictures are ugly and I don't like them.
你不要想改變我的看法。	And you're not going to change my mind.

vocabulary

represent [rɛprɪ'zɛnt]	代表
picture	圖畫
bowl [bol]	碗

orange		橘子
pear		梨子
necessary [ˈnɛsəˌsɛrɪ]		必須的
analysis [əˈnæləsɪs]		分析
joke [dʒok]		笑話
ugly		醜陋的

Unit 3

在圖書館

Dialog 1

Chapter 9

對不起，請問目錄卡在哪裡？	Excuse me, could you direct me to the card catalogue?
我們的目錄卡是電子的。	Our card catalogue is electronic.
你可以用角落的那部電腦去找。	You can access it with that computer in the corner.

電腦上面有使用說明嗎？	Does the computer have instructions on it?
有，那其實是很容易使用的。	Yes, it's really pretty easy to use.
好的，但是如果我不會用，我會回來請你幫忙。	Okay, but if I can't figure it out I'm going to come back and ask for your help.
我跟你一道過去，看你會使用我才離開。	I'll go with you and make sure you understand it.

Dialog 2

我不知道你是否能幫我找到這本書。	I was wondering if you could help me find this book.
『頑童流浪記』…有，我們應該有那本書。	The Adventures of Huckleberry Finn... yes, we should have that.
你有沒有查過目錄卡？	Have you checked the card catalogue?
說真的，我不識字。	Actually, I don't know how to read.

我是給我兒子借這本書。	I'm just getting the book for my son.
很抱歉。	I'm sorry.
我去拿這本書給你。	I'll get the book for you.
你知道我們星期三晚間有教認字的課吧？	You do know we have literacy classes on Wednesday night, don't you?
不，我不知道。	No, I didn't know that.
或許我下個星期三會來。	Maybe I'll come next Wednesday.
你應該來的。	You should.
這個社會上，每個人真的都需要會基本的讀寫。	Everyone in this society really needs to be literate.

vocabulary

direct [dəˈrɛkt]	給～指路
catalogue [ˈkætəlɔg]	目錄
electronic [ɪˈlɛktrɑnɪk]	電子的

access [ˈæksɛs]	使用
corner	角落
instructions [ɪnˈstrʌkʃənz]	用法說明
literacy [ˈlɪtərəsɪ]	讀寫能力
literate [ˈlɪtərɪt]	有讀寫能力的
society	社會

Unit 4

去演唱會

Dialog 1

先生，你不能帶著那個水桶進演唱會。	You can't come into the concert with that ice chest, sir.
但是冰桶裡有瓶裝的水。	But it has bottled water in it.
我可不想脫水。	I don't want to get dehydrated.

你可以在裡面買水喝。	You can buy water inside.
我不想花五塊錢買一杯水。	I don't want to spend five dollars on a cup of water.
請你讓我帶一些水進去。	Please let me bring some water with me.
先生，很抱歉。	I'm sorry, sir.
規定不准，讓你帶水或冰桶進去。	The rules forbid me from allowing you to bring an ice chest or bottled water.
我非常不高興。	I'm very upset.
我要跟負責的人談。	I want to talk to whoever is in charge.

Dialog 2

瑪麗，你興奮嗎？	Are you excited, Mary?
當然，我很興奮。	Of course I'm excited.

我已經四年沒有看『瑪丹娜』的演唱會了。	I haven't seen Modona in concert in four years.
是啊，我也很急著聽她新唱片裡所有的歌。	Yeah, I'm anxious to hear all the songs from her new album.
她的老歌仍然是最好的。	Her old songs are still the best, though.
我很高興我們有前排的位子。	I'm glad we have front row seats.
我們可以摸到舞台。	We'll be able to touch the stage.

vocabulary

concert ['kɑnsɚt]	演唱會
ice chest	冰桶
bottled water	瓶裝水
dehydrated [dɪ'haɪ,dretɪd]	脫水
rule	規則
forbid [fɚ'bɪd]	禁止
upset	不高興
in charge	負責
anxious ['æŋkʃəs]	急切的

album	唱片
front	前面
stage [stedʒ]	舞臺

Unit 5

課堂英語

Dialog 1

我等不急下課鈴響。	I can't wait for the bell to ring.
就是說嘛。	No kidding.
李老師說的好慢，我都快睡著了。	Mr. Lee's been talking so slowly I'm almost asleep.
糟糕，我想他聽到我們的談話了。	Whoops, I think he heard us.
沒有，他只是在看後面那個一直在睡覺的學生。	No, he was just looking at that kid who keeps falling asleep in the back.

Chapter 9

已經快三點了。	It's almost three o'clock.
鈴聲一響，我就要趕去搭公車。	I'm going to run for the bus as soon as the bell rings.
我打賭我會比你快坐上公車。	I bet I'll beat you to the bus.

Dialog 2

今天林老師派的家庭作業太多了。	Mr. Lin assigned way too much homework today.
是啊。	That's for sure.
我不知道怎麼找時間來做他的研究報告，又同時準備即將到來的期末考。	I don't know how I'll find time to do a research paper in his class and study for all the finals coming up.
何況我們星期六晚上還有舞會。	Plus we've got that party on Saturday night.
你知道的，湯姆舉辦的那一個。	You know, the one Tom's throwing.
喔，我都忘記了。	Oh man, I forgot about that.

我真希望沒有這些家庭作業。	I wish I didn't have all this homework.
是啊，學校實在是件令人討厭的事。	Yeah, school's a real drag.
至少，我們今年年底就要畢業了。	At least we'll be graduating at the end of the year.
那一定會令人很興奮。	That'll be so exciting.
我希望我能順利過關。	I hope I can make it.

vocabulary

bell	鈴聲
ring	（鈴聲）響
beat	贏
assign [ə'saɪn]	指定
research	研究
final ['faɪnl]	期末考
throwing a party	開宴會（throw 的現在分詞）
drag [dræg]	（俗話）極討厭的事
graduating ['grædʒʊ‚etɪŋ]	畢業（graduate 的現在分詞）

MEMO

Chapter 10 球類比賽和運動

....

Unit 1

高爾夫球

Dialog 1

約翰，你上一洞打了幾桿？	What did you get on that last hole, John?
我打了平標準桿。	I got par.
那是我整場球第一個標準桿。	It's the first par I've had all game.
你記得為球出界加上一桿嗎？	Did you remember to add a stroke for going out of bounds?
哎呀，我忘了。	Oh, I forgot about that.
我想我又得了個『柏忌』。	I guess I got another bogey.

好啊，那是說我們仍然平手。	Well, that means we're still tied.
接下來這一洞，你要不要賭一點錢，增添樂趣？	Do you want to wager a little money on this next hole, just to make things interesting?

Dialog 2

我最痛恨球掉在沙坑裡。	I hate landing in the sand trap!
現在為了把球打出沙坑我可能得浪費幾桿了。	Now I'm probably going to waste strokes trying to get out.
至少妳還沒把球打進水裡。	At least you haven't landed in the water yet.
我上兩洞都掉進水裡了呢！	I've done that on the last two holes.
請把我的挖桿遞給我。	Could you hand me my wedge?
我要試著把球敲進洞去。	I'm going to try to chip this into the hole.

在這兒，給你！	Here you go.
我等你上了果嶺再推桿。	I'll wait for you to get on the green before I putt.
不用，你先推桿吧。	No, you go ahead and putt out.
然後我才打。	Then I'll go.
我才不要這樣呢，瑪麗小姐。	No way, Mary.
我要讓妳先打。	I'm going to let you go first.
我才不要先推桿的壓力。	I don't want the pressure of putting first.

vocabulary

hole	（高爾夫球）球穴
par [pɑr]	（高爾夫球）標準桿
stroke [strok]	擊出一球
bogey ['bogɪ]	（高爾夫球）柏忌；超過標準桿一桿
tie	平分
wager ['wedʒɚ]	打賭
wedge [wɛdʒ]	（高爾夫球）挖桿

chip	（高爾夫球）觸擊
putt	（高爾夫球）推桿
pressure [ˈprɛʃɚ]	壓力

Unit 2

籃球

Dialog 1

妳要不要來打一場球。	Do you feel like playing with one?
當然。	Sure.
不過，我打得不太好。	I'm not very good, though.
沒有關係。	That's all right.
咱們只是打著玩的。	We're just playing for fun.

你要先攻？	Do you want the ball first?
咱們來投籃決定。	Let's shoot for it.
先投進的人先攻。	Whoever gets the first basket gets the ball.
好吧，誰要先投？	Okay, who should shoot first?

Dialog 2

你那個動作我得抓你犯規。	I'm going to have to call foul on that play.
你說什麼？	What do you mean?
我可沒觸犯妳。	I didn't foul you.
我要投籃的時候，你碰著我的手肘了。	You hit my elbow when I was shooting.
那是犯規的。	That's a foul.
妳的手肘碰到我的頭。	You hit your elbow on my head.

要是有人犯規的話，那人是妳。	If anyone fouled, it was you.
好了、好了！	OK.
算啦！	Just forget it.
反正你從來也沒公平地玩過球。	You never play fair anyway.
別假惺惺了。	No.
投吧，妳儘管罰球吧。	Go ahead and take your free throw.
我知道妳得靠作弊贏球。	I understand that you have to cheat to win.

vocabulary

shoot	（籃球）投籃
foul [faʊl]	（籃球）犯規
elbow [ˈɛlˌbo]	手肘
fair	公平的
cheat	欺騙
win	贏球

棒球

Dialog 1

你認為我應該投給他快速球嗎？	Do you think I should give him my fast ball?
我想不太好吧。	I don't know.
這個傢伙已經打了兩個全壘打，也許我們應該保送他上壘。	This guy's already hit two home runs, maybe we should walk him.
不行，我可以讓他出局。	No way, I can get him out.
再給我一次機會吧。	Just give me another chance.
約翰，這個傢伙很危險。	John, this guy's dangerous.
他可以重槌你的球。	He can hit that ball a ton.
我們不能冒這個險。	We can't chance it.

哎呀，教練，我要投曲球給他。	Look, coach, I'll throw him curve balls.
我們不能輕易保送他。	We can't just walk him.
好吧。	All right.
命運全在你手上。	It's in your hands.
小心一點。	Just be careful.

Dialog 2

這是我整個球季所參觀過紐約洋基隊最好的一場比賽。	This is the best Yankee's game I've been to all season!
真的！	No kidding.
我從沒見過他們打這麼多全壘打。	I've never seen them hit so many homers.
還有，投手也很來勁。	And the pitcher's on fire.
他從來沒有投那麼好。	He's never pitched so well.

啊，彼得要上場打擊了。	Oh, Peter is up to bat.
他是我最喜歡的球員。	He's my favorite.
我想他這場球還沒被三振過。	I don't think he's struck out yet this game.
沒有，他每次打擊都打出安打。	No, he's gotten a hit at every bat.
這場比賽太妙了！	What a game!

vocabulary

home run	（棒球）全壘打
walk	（棒球）保送上壘
dangerous [ˈdendʒərəs]	危險的
coach [kotʃ]	教練
curve ball	（棒球）曲球
homer [ˈhomɚ]	（棒球）全壘打
pitcher [ˈpɪtʃɚ]	投手
bat	（棒球）打擊
is struck out	被三振出局

網球

Dialog 1

零比二。	Love-thirty.
第二次發球。	Second serve.
準備好了沒有？	Are you ready?
準備好了。這次給我發個好球。	Yeah, give me a good serve this time.
我看你二發失敗，看得都煩了。	I'm tired of watching you get double-faults.
哎呀，你得了吧。	Hey, give me a break.
網球最難就在發球。	Serving is the toughest part of the game.
你就是需要多多練習。	You just need to practice more.

我一直都在練習我的發球。	I practice my serve all the time.
可是我總是觸網。	But I always hit the net.
也許你應該去上網球課。	Maybe you should take tennis lessons.
我就是這樣做的。	That's what I did.

Dialog 2

球出界了。	It's out.
球差點就進，不過它肯定是出了界。	It was almost in, but it's definitely out.
你確定嗎？	Are you sure?
從我的角度看，那個球看起來是好球。	From my angle that shot looked good.
那很難說。	It's hard to tell.
我真的認為球出界了。	I really think the ball was out.

唔⋯，我真的認為球是在界內的。	Well, I really think the ball was in.
好吧，咱們重新發球再打這一分如何？	Ok, how about if we just serve the ball over again and replay the point?
可以，這聽起來還算公道。	Yeah, that sounds fair to me.

vocabulary

love-thirty	（網球）零比三十；零對二球
serve	（網球）發球
double-fault	（網球）兩次發球失誤
toughest ['tʌfɪst]	最困難的
practice ['præktɪs]	練習
net	球網
definitely ['dɛfənɪtlɪ]	肯定地
angle ['æŋgl̩]	角度
replay	重打
point	分數

美式足球

Dialog 1

哇！真不敢相信湯姆衝破所有的防衛線。	Wow, can you believe Tom broke all those tackles?
他這個球員真的很強。	He's a really strong player.
我見過別人只能跑幾碼的情況下，他卻跑了二十碼。	I've seen him go twenty yards when a normal man could only have gone two.
是啊，他是很強的跑鋒。	Yeah, he's a strong runner.
要是我去防衛他，我會很不喜歡。	I'd hate to have to tackle him.
我要是像那些人一樣有三百磅的肌肉，我大概也會是很好的足球員。	If I had 300 pounds of muscle like most of those guys do, I'd probably be a good football player.

你要是有三百磅的肌肉，我大概會很怕你。	If you had 300 pounds of muscle, I would probably be scared of you.
是啊，足球員是很嚇人的。	Yeah. Football players are scary.

Dialog 2

第三次攻球，還要攻八碼才行。	Third down, 8 yards to go.
好緊張噢！	What a tense moment.
我說我們得擲球到中央位置。	I say we go with a deep pass right down the center.
那不太好。	I don't know.
那有些冒險。	That's kind of risky.
我們要是沒接到，就得踢給他們進攻了。	If I miss the throw, we'll have to punt.
哎呀，怕則不能成事嘛！	Hey, no guts no glory.

至少，我們要試試。	We have to try, at the least.
你可以跑得很快嗎？	Can you run fast?
因為我擲球之前無法等太久噢。	Because I'm not going to be able to wait very long before throwing.
別擔心。	Don't worry.
用力擲球，其他一切包在我身上。	Just throw it hard and leave the rest up to me.

vocabulary

tackle ['tækl̩]	（足球）阻截對方球員
yard	碼
runner ['rʌnɚ]	帶球進攻的球員
muscle ['mʌsl̩]	肌肉
scary ['skɛrɪ]	令人害怕的
tense	緊張的
moment	時刻
risky	冒險的
throw	投球
punt [pʌnt]	（足球）踢凌空球/進攻失敗踢球
guts	膽量
glory ['glorɪ]	榮譽

游泳

你是游蝶式嗎？	Was that the butterfly you were doing?
不，我都用蛙式。	No, I was using the breast stroke.
兩樣看起來都很類似。	They look very similar.
我想是吧。	I suppose they do.
我較喜歡蛙式，因為蛙式用力較少。	I like the breast stroke better than the butterfly because it uses less energy.
你可以教我蛙式嗎？	Could you teach me the breast stroke?
可以，那不難學的。	Sure, it's not very difficult to learn.

你要不要比賽。	Do you want to race?
哎呀,約翰,我知道你比我快得多。	Oh, I know you're a lot faster than me, John.
我才不要比賽呢。	I don't want to race.
你不敢?	Are you a chicken?
你怕什麼嘛?	What are you so afraid of?
約翰,我根本不會游泳。	I don't know how to swim, John.
很抱歉。	I'm sorry.
我不知道是這樣。	I didn't realize that.
我以為人人都會游泳。	I thought everyone knew how to swim.
從來沒人教我,所以我從來沒學。	No one ever taught me, so I never learned.

butterfly
['bʌtɚ,flaɪ]
（游泳）蝶式

breast
[brɛst]
胸部

stroke
[strok]
撲打

breast stroke
（游泳）蛙式

similar
['sɪmələ]
類似的

energy
['ɛnɚdʒɪ]
力氣

race
比賽

chicken
膽小鬼

swim
游泳

realize
['riə,laɪz]
知道

Chapter 11 談電腦

Unit 1

個人電腦

Dialog 1

用五百塊美金買一部二手的『IBM個人電腦』是好價錢嗎？	Is five hundred dollars a good price for a used IBM PC?
那要看情形，是多舊的？	That depends, how old is it?
是Pentium『奔騰』的。	It's a Pentium.
所以我想應該不會太舊。	So I suppose it's not very old.
是的，它很可能是兩年左右的。	Yeah, it's probably about two years old.

有沒有光碟機？	Does it have a CD ROM?
有的，我想有。	Yes, I think it does.
它還有Super VGA 的顯示器。	It also has a Super VGA monitor.
嗯，那麼我想那可能是一個合理的價錢。	Well, I think that's probably a reasonable price, then.
要是我的話，我會買的。	I'd buy it.

Dialog 2

你的電腦上有沒有視窗95？	Do you have Windows 95 on your PC?
有的，我想每一個人最終都會裝上視窗95。	Yeah, I figured everyone was going to get it eventually.
所以我也裝了。	So I got it, too.
你喜歡它嗎？	Do you like it very much?

還好。	It's all right.
但是，程式上還有一些小錯誤，令我很煩惱。	But there are little bugs in the program that bother me.
我知道你的意思。	I know what you mean.
出問題的都是小毛病。	Little things will go wrong.
那樣子會使得整個程式看起來很糟糕。	And it makes the whole program seem bad.
嗯，每一個程式總免不了會有一些錯誤。	Oh well, every program is bound to have some bugs.
那是不可避免的。	It's inevitable.

vocabulary

price	價格
used	用過的；舊的
depend [dɪˈpɛnd]	依～而決定
monitor [ˈmɑnətɚ]	電腦顯示器

Chapter 11

reasonable [ˈriznəbl̩]	合理的
figure [ˈfɪgjɚ]	（口語）明白
eventually [ɪˈvɛntʃʊəlɪ]	最終的
bug	電腦軟體的錯誤
bother [ˈbɑðɚ]	使惱怒
is bound to	免不了有
inevitable [ɪnˈɛvɪtəbl̩]	不能避免的

Unit 2

電腦遊戲

Dialog 1

你買了『WarCraft 二代』沒有？	Have you bought WarCraft 2 yet?
買了！它發行的當天我就買了。	Yeah! I bought it the day it was released.
你喜歡嗎？	How do you like it?

這個電腦遊戲很棒。	It's a great game.
有很多新的角色。	There are a lot of new characters.
很貴嗎？	Did it cost very much?
它賣三十美元左右。	It cost about thirty bucks.
大部份的電腦遊戲差不多都是這個價錢。	Most games cost about that much.

Dialog 2

電腦遊戲『麥可戰士』真好玩。	Mechwarrior is such a good game.
畫面棒極了！	The graphics are awesome!
哦，我知道你的意思。	Oh, I know what you mean.
我已經迷上了那個遊戲。	I'm addicted to that game.

我的室友總是想要玩。	My roommate always wants to play it.
但是我叫她自己去買一個。	But I told her to buy her own game.
是嗎，我的室友喜歡看我玩。	Yeah, my roommate likes to watch me play.
他說好像在看電影一樣。	He says it's like watching a movie.
我沒有看過這麼好的畫面。	I've never seen such good graphics.
我也沒有聽過電腦遊戲裡有這麼好的音樂。	And I've never heard such good sound in a game.

vocabulary

released [rɪ'list]		發行（release的過去分詞）
character ['kærɪktɚ]		人物；角色
buck		元（一塊錢）
graphic ['græfɪk]		圖／畫面
awesome ['ɔsəm]		令人嘆為觀止
addicted [ə'dɪktɪd]		沈迷的（addict的過去分詞）

Unit 3

Internet 網路

Dialog 1

你最近有沒有上網路？	Have you surfed the net lately?
很少。	Not very much.
我的數據機很慢。	My modem's slow.
我也沒有耐心等全部東西都讀取完畢。	And I don't have the patience to wait for everything to load.
圖畫會使所有的東西慢下來。	Pictures really slow things down.
如果只看文字會比較快一點。	It's quicker to surf in text-only mode.
真的嗎？我要試試這麼做。	Really? I'll have to try that.

反正我也不需要圖畫。	I don't need the pictures anyway.
是啊，我通常只是找一些資料。	Yeah, I'm usually just looking up information.
所以圖畫並不是那麼重要。	So pictures aren't that important.
反正大部份的圖畫都只是廣告。	Most of the pictures are just advertisements anyway.

Dialog 2

遊戲園區的ｗｅｂ ｐａｇｅ首頁真的很棒。	The Gameland web page is really cool.
我不知道遊戲園區有web page。	I didn't know Gameland has a web page.
每一個人都有ｗｅｂ page。	Everybody has a web page.
你只是需要去找。	You just have to find it.

你怎麼找到每一樣東西？	How can you find anything, though?
嗯，如果你沒有地址的話，可以用搜尋引擎去找。	Well, if you don't have an address you can just use the search engines to find places.
我可得要試著用搜尋引擎。	I'll have to try using the search engines.

vocabulary

surfed [sɜ·ft]	上網路
modem ['mɔdəm]	數據機
patience	耐心
load	讀取
mode	狀態
advertisement [ædvɚ'taɪzmənt]	廣告
search	搜尋
engine ['ɛndʒən]	引擎
search engine	搜尋引擎

電子郵件

Dialog 1

約翰，你大學畢業以後我會想念你。	I'm going to miss you when you leave college, John.
我們還可以寫信。	We can still write.
我知道，但是寫信很慢。	I know, but writing is so slow.
我不知道我有沒有耐心。	I don't know if I'll have the patience.
不，我的意思是我們可以互相用電子郵件通信。	No, I mean we can E-mail each other.
那樣的話，既快又便宜。	It's quick and cheap.

你是說你大學畢業以後，還會繼續用原來電子郵件的地址嗎？

You mean you'll still have your E-mail address when you leave college?

是的，學校讓校友在畢業以後，仍然保有他們的地址。

Yes, the school let alumni keep their address even after they graduate.

Dialog 2

你有沒有收到史蒂夫寄的電子郵件？

Did you get that E-mail from Steve?

有的，我想每一個人都收到了。

Yes, I think everybody did.

那個渾球寄給整個辦公室的人。

The jerk sent it to the whole office.

他們把他開除了嗎？

Did they fire him?

我想是的。

I think so.

寫一些很沒禮貌的東西，並且把它寄給每一個人是很愚蠢的事情。	It was pretty stupid of him to write something so rude and send it to everybody.
我猜老闆不太高興。	I bet the boss wasn't too happy.
他是不高興。	He wasn't.
他打算在星期五讓我們聽一個講習會，講有關使用電子郵件的規矩。	He's going to make us sit through a seminar about E-mail etiquette on Friday.

vocabulary

miss	想念
alumni [ə'lʌmnaɪ]	畢業生（alumnus 的複數）
graduate ['grædʒʊˌet]	畢業
jerk	（口語）渾球
fire	開除
rude [rud]	沒禮貌
seminar ['sɛmɪnɑr]	講習會
etiquette ['ɛtɪˌkɛt]	規矩；道德

Chapter 12

在餐廳

Unit 1

點菜

| Dialog 1 |

你們今天有什麼特餐嗎？	Do you have any specials today?
燒烤雞，另外附加蛋花湯。	The Teriyaki Chicken with a side order of egg drop soup.
聽起來很不錯。	That sounds excellent.
我就點那一個。	I'll have that.
你要喝什麼嗎？	Would you like anything to drink with that?
你們有百事可樂嗎？	Do you have Pepsi?

如果沒有，我就喝可口可樂。	If not, I'll have Coke.
有的，我們有百事可樂。	Yes, we have Pepsi.
我馬上拿來給你。	I'll bring that right out.

Dialog 2

各位可以點菜了嗎？	Are you folks ready to order yet?
我想我們還需要幾分鐘。	I think we need a few more minutes.
好的，你們要點菜的時候告訴我一聲。	Okay, just let me know when you're ready.
請等一下。	Just a minute.
你們今天的特別菜是什麼？	What is your vegetable of the day?
今天的特別菜是甜酸雞。	Today it's sweet & sour chicken.
我不喜歡雞。	I don't like chicken.

| 多給我們幾分鐘做決定。 | Give us a few more minutes to decide. |

vocabulary

special [ˈspɛʃəl]	特餐
egg drop soup	蛋花湯
folk [fok]	（口語）各位
vegetable [ˈvɛdʒtəbl]	蔬菜
decide	決定
sweet & sour chicken	甜酸雞

Unit 2

飯後甜點

Dialog 1

| 一切還好嗎？ | How was everything? |

| 很好！ | It was great! |

還吃得下甜點嗎？	Any room for dessert?
嗯，你們有什麼甜點？	Well, what do you have?
幾乎你要什麼都有。	Just about anything you could want.
你要我拿甜點盤過來嗎？	Should I show you our dessert tray?
好的。我想要看看哪一樣看起來最好吃。	Yes. I want to see which one looks the tastiest.

Dialog 2

這是我們的甜點盤。	This is our dessert tray.
那一個是什麼？	What's that one?
那是起司蛋糕。	This is cheesecake.
你們有沒有上面放草莓的？	Do you have any strawberry topping?
我不喜歡桃子！	I hate peach!

有的，我們有！	Yes, we sure do!
那麼我要上面放草莓的起司蛋糕，不要桃子的。	Then I'll have the cheesecake with strawberry topping instead of peach.

vocabulary

dessert [dɪˈzɝt]	甜點
tray [tre]	盤子
tastiest [ˈtestɪst]	最好吃的
topping [ˈtɑpɪŋ]	糕點上的裝飾配料

Unit 3

付帳

Dialog 1

甜點好吃嗎？	Did you enjoy dessert?

哦，很好吃！	Oh, it was wonderful!
我希望所有的食物都是甜點！	I wish all food was dessert!
我很高興你喜歡。	I'm glad you liked it.
帳單在這兒。	Here's the check.
我直接付給你嗎？	Do I pay you directly?
是的。等你準備好我就可以幫你結帳。	Yes. I'll take care of that whenever you're ready.
謝謝你。	Thank you.

Dialog 2

對不起，我要付帳了。	Excuse me, I'm ready to pay.
哦，好的。	Oh, all right.
我不需要找零錢。	I don't need any change.
好的，先生。謝謝你。	Okay, sir. Thank you.
我非常喜歡這一頓飯。	I enjoyed this meal thoroughly.

很謝謝你！	Thank you so much!
哦，不用客氣！	Oh, you're certainly welcome!
再來！	Come back soon!

vocabulary

food	食物
check	帳單
pay	付帳
directly [dəˈrɛktlɪ]	直接的
thoroughly [ˈθɝolɪ]	徹頭徹尾的

Unit 4
在麥當勞點餐

Dialog 1

先生，你要什麼嗎？	Can I help you, sir?

嗯，我要三號套餐。	Yes, I'll have the number three combo.
你要什麼汽水？	What type of soda do you want?
我想我要可樂。	I guess I'll have Coke.
先生，你的餐點要加大嗎？	Would you like to Super Size your meal, sir?
不，不需要。	No, that's all right.
我想我吃不完那麼多薯條。	I don't think I can eat that many French fries.

Dialog 2

歡迎光臨『麥當勞』。	Welcome to McDonald's.
你要點什麼？	Can I take your order?
嗨，我要一個漢堡和一個蘋果派。	Hi, I'd like a Hamburger and an apple pie.
你要在這兒吃呢，還是外帶？	Will that be for here or to go?

我在這兒吃。	I'll eat it here.
還有，能多放一些蕃茄醬在漢堡上嗎？	And can I get extra ketchup on that Hamburger?
可以的，總共是四塊三毛六美金。	Sure, that'll be $4.36.
這是五塊錢。	Here's a five.
我可以多要幾張紙巾嗎？	Could I have extra napkins, too?

vocabulary

combo	套餐
type	種類
soda	汽水
French fries	薯條
order	點菜
apple pie	蘋果派
extra [ˈɛkstrə]	多餘的
ketchup	蕃茄醬
napkin [ˈnæpkɪn]	紙巾

用餐

Dialog 1

你要去『肯德基炸雞』還是『漢堡王』?	Do you want to go to KFC or Burger King?
『麥當勞』怎麼樣?	What about McDonald's?
我們老是去那裡。	We always go there.
讓我們試試其它不同的。	Let's try something different.
嗯,我喜歡『肯德基炸雞』店的沙拉吧。	Well, I like KFC's salad bar.
是啊,他們有烤馬鈴薯,我很喜歡。	Yeah, they have baked potatoes, too, which I like.

好，看起來我們兩個都想去『肯德基炸雞』店。	OK, it looks like we both want to go to KFC's.

Dialog 2

你要吃光所有的薯條嗎？	Are you going to eat all of those fries?
不，你可以拿去吃。	No, you can go ahead and have them.
你如果吃不完，為什麼每次你都是買特大號的？	Why do you Super Size your meal if you can't eat it all?
我不知道。	I don't know.
我想我總是認為我的胃口很大，實際上卻不是。	I guess I always think my appetite is bigger than it really is.
我可沒關係。	I don't mind.
那樣我還佔便宜，可以吃多一些。	That means I get to eat more.

是啊，你要是繼續吃別人和自己的食物，你吃得多也變得胖。

Yeah, and you're going to get fat, too, if you keep eating other people's food as well as your own.

Chapter 13 在百貨公司

Unit 1

買香水

Dialog 1

你要不要試試我們的新香水？	Would you like to try our new perfume?
不要把它噴在我的身上。	Don't spray that on me.
為什麼？	Why?
我不喜歡身上聞起來有好幾種香味。	I hate smelling like more than one fragrance.
好的，小姐。我道歉。	Okay, ma'am. I apologize.
沒關係。	That's quite all right.

嗨。我想買東西給我女兒。	Hi. I'm shopping for my daughter.
生日嗎？	Birthday?
不，是畢業。	No, graduation.
我們有一個特別的禮盒只賣二十四塊九毛九。	We have this special gift package for $24.99.
那禮盒包括些什麼？	What does that include?
一個可愛的旅行用化妝盒、香皂，還有三盎司香水。	A lovely travel case, soap, and three ounces of perfume.

vocabulary

perfume [ˈpɝfjum]		香水
spray [spre]		噴灑
smelling [ˈsmɛlɪŋ]	聞起來（smell 的動名詞）	
fragrance [ˈfrægrəns]		香味
apologize [əˈpɑləˌdʒaɪz]		道歉

birthday [ˈbɝθˌde]		生日
graduation [ˌgrædʒʊˈeʃən]		畢業
gift package		禮盒
ounce [ɑns]		盎司
travel case		旅行用化妝盒

Unit 2

買鞋子

Dialog 1

你需要我幫忙嗎？	Is there something I can help you with?
是的，我女兒需要一雙銀色的鞋子。	Yes, my daughter needs silver shoes.
畢業舞會的季節。	Prom season.
每一個人都需要特定的鞋子。	Everyone needs a specific shoe.

是啊。她穿高跟鞋不太會走路。	Yes. She can't walk in heels very well.
那她就不應該去參加畢業舞會。	Then she shouldn't be going to Prom.
哈哈，銀色的鞋子在哪裡？	Ha, ha. Where are the silver shoes?

Dialog 2

我們通常不按顏色來安排，而是按照設計師。	We don't normally organize by color, but by designer.
最便宜的設計師的鞋子放哪兒？	How about the cheapest designer?
如果你是考慮價錢，你可能要到清倉架去看看。	You might try looking at the clearance rack if that's what you're concerned about.
她穿十二號鞋。	She's a size 12.

在你們這兒我卻找不到那個尺寸。	I didn't even find that size here.
那可能是因為較大尺碼都已經賣光了。	That's probably because all the larger sizes have already been sold.
好像大號的鞋子跑得快似的！	Big shoes must go fast!

vocabulary

silver shoes	銀色的鞋子
prom	畢業舞會
season [ˈsizn̩]	季節
specific [spɪˈsɪfɪk]	特定的
heels	鞋跟
organize [ˈɔrgənˌaɪz]	安排
designer [dɪˈzaɪnɚ]	設計師
clearance [ˈklɪrəns]	清倉
rack	架子

買珠寶

Dialog 1

爸爸，我要這邊這一個。	Dad, I want this right here.
那是鑽戒！	That's a diamond ring!
買給我吧。	Buy it for me.
很抱歉，你不需我買鑽戒給你。	Sorry, you don't need a diamond ring from me.
那麼，我幾時才能得到鑽戒？	Well, when will I ever get one?
找個男朋友。	Find a man.
然後再來操心鑽戒的事！	Then worry about the diamond rings!

Dialog 2

親愛的，這個戒子你覺得怎麼樣？	Honey, what do you think about this band?
給我還是給你的？	For me or you?
給我的。	For me.
我不喜歡。	I don't like it.
為什麼？	Why?
它看起來很男性化，一點都不女性化。	It's just so manly, not very feminine.

vocabulary

diamond [ˈdaɪəmənd]	鑽石的
ring	戒指
find	找到
band [bænd]	（扁平不鑲大寶石的）戒指
feminine [ˈfɛmənɪn]	女性的

買化妝品

Dialog 1

嗨，你需要我幫忙嗎？	Hi, is there something special I can do?
我只是需要買一些新的眼影。	I just need to buy some eye shadow.
你需要什麼顏色的？	What color do you need?
淡一點，但是中性的顏色。	Light but neutral colors.
這一個你擦起來會很好看。	This one would look nice on you.
多少錢？	How much is it?

Dialog 2

十五元。	It's fifteen.

好的，我買。	Okay, I'll take it.
還要買其它的東西嗎？	Will there be anything else?
不，我想這樣就夠了。	No, I think that does it.
你要用希爾斯的卡簽帳嗎？	Will this be on your Sear's card?
不，我要付現金。	No, it's cash.

vocabulary

eye shadow	眼影
neutral ['njutrəl]	中性的
cash	現金

Unit 5

其他附件

Dialog 1

| 我在找黑色或者是深棕色的皮包。 | I'm looking for either a black or dark brown purse. |

瑪麗，這一個怎麼樣？	How about this one, Mary?
不。我不喜歡那個質料。	No. I hate that texture.
這個很漂亮，但是很貴。	This one's pretty, but it costs too much.
多少錢？	How much?
兩千美元。	Two thousand.

Dialog 2

是很貴，那遠超出我的預算。	Yes, that is way more than I wanted to spend.
這一個怎麼樣？	How about this one?
我沒辦法把我所有的東西都放進去！	I could never fit all my things in that!
那妳要多大的？	How big do you need it to be?

至少要跟我的那個舊的一樣大，但可能要不同的樣式。	At least as big as my old one, but maybe a different style.
妳那個舊的何不再使用一段時間？	Why don't you just use your old one for a while?

vocabulary

dark brown
深棕色

purse
[pɝs]
皮包

texture
['tɛkstʃɚ]
質地

style
[staɪl]
形式

fit
容納

MEMO

Chapter 14

購物

unit 1

付款

Dialog 1

嗨。我已經準備好要結帳。	Hi. I'm ready to check out.
我馬上過來。	I'll be right with you.
我在趕時間。	I'm kind of in a hurry.
先生，對不起。	I'm sorry, sir.
請等一下。	Just one moment.
我可沒整天的時間等你！	I haven't got all day!
好的，先生。	Okay, sir.

我可以幫你結帳了。	I'm ready.

謝謝你這麼迅速。	Thanks for being so prompt.
這一個是在清倉架上的嗎？	Was this on the clearance rack?
是的，是打五折。	Yes, it was 50% off.
好的。你要用現金、支票，還是用信用卡？	Okay. Will this be cash, check, or charge?
用信用卡。你們收Master卡嗎？	Charge. Do you accept Master Card?
先生，我們收。	Yes, sir.

vocabulary

check out	結帳
in a hurry	匆忙的
ready ['rɛdɪ]	準備好
prompt [prɑmpt]	迅速的

Unit 2

退貨

Dialog 1

嗨。我的老闆派我來退還這些東西。	Hi. My boss sent me to return these.
壞了嗎？	Is it broken?
我不知道。	I don't know.
她只是說:『把這個拿去還。』	She just said, "Return this."
嗯。好吧。	Hmm. Okay.
這張收據她還要嗎？	Does she want the receipt back?

| 我想是吧。 | I believe so. |

嗨，我把電燈一打開，這個燈泡就爆炸了。	Hi. This bulb exploded when I turned the lamp on.
你用手指頭去碰它了嗎？	Did you touch it with your fingers?
沒有，我按照說明是用紙巾去拿的。	No, I did just as I was told and used a tissue.
那它還是爆炸了？	And it still exploded?
你的電燈可能有短路。	There might be a short in the lamp.
我想不可能。	I don't think so.
我另外再給你一個。	I'll give you another one.
如果還是爆炸，把電燈拿來讓我們檢查一下。	If it happens again, bring the lamp in so we can check it out.

vocabulary

boss [bɔs]	老闆
return	退還
believe	相信
bulb [bʌlb]	燈泡
exploded [ɪksˈplodɪd]	爆炸（explode 的過去式）
lamp	燈
finger [ˈfɪŋɚ]	手指
tissue [ˈtɪʃu]	紙巾
short	（電器等）短路

Unit 3

包禮物

Dialog 1

這些我需要包起來。　　I need these wrapped.

我正要去參加一個給新娘送禮物的聚會。	I'm on my way to a bridal shower.
我們只免費包裝第一項物品。	The free gift wrap is for the first item only.
好的，那麼就免費包這個大的。	Okay, wrap the large one for free, then.
其它的我付錢。	I'll pay for the others.
我要用這種包裝紙。	I'll use this gift wrap.
好。	That's fine.
你能不能讓手柄留在包裝紙外？	Can you leave the handle sticking out of the wrapping?
不行。	No.

Dialog 2

不行？為什麼不行？	No? Why not?
我就是辦不到。	I just can't.
那我要怎麼攜帶？	How am I supposed to carry it?
我們可以派一個人幫你拿到車上。	We can have someone help you to your car.
不行，我還得能從我的車子拿出來才可以。	No, I need to be able to carry it out of my car as well.
嗯，如果你一定要這樣，我們可以在手柄附近留個大口。	Well, we can leave a big hole around the handle if you insist.
但包裹上我就不貼本店的標籤了。	But I'm not putting a store sticker on that package.
因為那樣子會讓我們公司形象很難看！	Because it will make us look bad!

right away
立刻

wrapped
[ræpt]
包起來（wrap 的過去分詞）

item
[ˈaɪtəm]
項目

wrap
包裝

handle
[ˈhændl̩]
把手

sticking
伸出（stick 的現在分詞）

carry
拿

hole
口；孔

insist
堅持

sticker
[ˈstɪkɚ]
貼紙；標籤

Chapter
15

MP3-16

在超級市場

Unit 1

問東西放在哪裡？

Dialog 1

奶油在哪裡？	Where is butter?
讓我查查看。	Let me check.
我看過牛奶的附近，但是不在那兒。	I looked near milk but it was nowhere.
它不會放在牛奶附近的。	It wouldn't be near milk.
我已經知道了。	I already knew that.
它是放在第十排貨架，冰淇淋的附近。	It's on aisle 10, near ice cream.

你們賣鮮肉嗎？	Do you carry fresh meat?
在後面的架子上我們有預裝好的肉。	We have pre-packaged meats at the back.
我是指有沒有人能給我現秤。	I mean like where someone measures it for me.
平常你可以到肉品部，叫我們的肉販秤給你，但現在肉品部打烊了。	You could normally go to the meat department and have our butcher do it for you, but it's closed.
肉品部幾時開始營業？	When is it open?
每天早上八點到下午八點。	From 8 to 8 every day.

vocabulary

butter [ˈbʌtɚ]	奶油
aisle [aɪl]	走道；行列
fresh	新鮮的
meat	肉
pre-packaged	預先裝好的

measure ['mɛʒɚ]	秤
department [dɪ'pɑrtmənt]	部門
butcher ['bʊtʃɚ]	肉販

Unit 2

在熟食部

Dialog 1

嗨，你要買什麼？	Hi, how can I help you?
我要四分之一磅燻火雞。	I need a quarter of a pound of smoked turkey.
好的，小姐。	Yes, ma'am.
還要半磅起司。	And a half pound of cheese.
好。	Yes.
還要半磅馬鈴薯沙拉。	And a half pound of potato salad.

就買這些嗎？	Will that be all?
不。我還要四分之一磅火腿。	No. I also would like a quarter pound of ham.
不過我要切成非常薄的薄片。	But I want it in very thin slices.
就這些嗎？	Is that all?
是。	Yes.
喏，給你。	Here you go.
謝謝。	Thank you very much!

vocabulary

quarter ['kwɔrtɚ]		四分之一
smoked		燻的
turkey		火雞
slice [slaɪs]		片

Chapter 16　在藥房

Unit 1

依處方開藥

Dialog 1

有什麼事嗎？	Yes, can I help you?
我有一張林醫師開的處方要拿藥。	I have a prescription from doctor Lin that needs to be filled.
讓我看看！	May I see it?
好，在這兒。	Yes, here.
天啊，這好難讀！	Boy, this is hard to read!
是啊，醫生們似乎很喜歡用很糟糕的筆跡寫字！	Yes, doctors seem to delight in horrible handwriting!

好，你要在這兒等，或者待會再來拿？	Okay, will you be waiting here or picking it up later?
我待會再來拿。	I'll pick it up.
好，沒問題。	Okay, that's fine.
你大約幾點再來？	About what time will you return?
大約六點。	About 6 o'clock.

vocabulary

prescription [prɪˈskrɪpʃən]		處方
filled [fɪld]	依處方開藥（fill 的過去分詞）	
hard		困難的
delight [dɪˈlaɪt]		喜歡
horrible [ˈhɔrəbl̩]		很糟的
handwriting [ˈhændˌraɪtɪŋ]		筆跡

unit 2

詢問

Dialog 1

對不起,你可以幫我一個忙嗎?	Excuse me, I was wondering if you could help me.
可以的。	Certainly.
我的女兒得了流行感冒。	My daughter has the flu.
我需要一些成藥。	And I need some over-the-counter medicine.
她幾歲?	How old is she?

Dialog 2

她只有六歲。	She's only 6.
她會吞藥丸嗎?	Can she swallow pills?

不會。	No.

是嗎？	Well, then.

我建議妳買些她吞得下的東西，例如液體藥品。	I suggest you buy something that she can swallow, like a liquid medicine.

這個可以治好感冒症狀嗎？	Would this one take care of flu symptoms?

可以。如果兩天內沒好，你再回來告訴我她的情況。	Yes. If it doesn't within 2 days, come back in and tell me about her condition.

vocabulary

certainly	當然
flu	流行 感冒
over-the-counter medicine	成藥
medicine ['mɛdəsn̩]	藥
swallow ['swɑlo]	吞食
pill	藥丸
liquid ['lɪkwɪd]	液體的
symptom ['sɪmptəm]	症狀
condition [kənˈdɪʃən]	情況

Chapter 17

在美容院

Unit 1

做頭髮

Dialog 1

嗨，我是瑪麗。	Hi, I'm Mary.
你有事先預約嗎？	Do you have an appointment?
有的，約好讓珍妮做。	Yes, with Jenny.
是約兩點鐘嗎？	2 o'clock?
是的。	Yes.
是林瑪麗嗎？	Mary Lin?
我就是。	That's me.

到後面去拿一個號碼。	Just go on back and take a number.
他們會先給你洗頭。	And they'll do your shampoo.
好的，謝謝。	Okay, thanks.
不用客氣。	You're welcome.

appointment [ə'pɔɪntmənt]　　　　　　約好時間

shampoo [ʃæm'pu]　　　　　　　　　　洗頭

Unit 2

剪頭髮

Dialog 1

嗨。我需要剪頭髮。	Hi. I need a haircut.

你有事先預約嗎？	Do you have an appointment?
沒有。	No.
嗯，我們三點十五好像有空。	Well, it looks like we have an opening at 3:15.
現在幾點？	What time is it now?
現在是兩點五十。	It's 2:50.

Chapter 17

Dialog 2

我就用那個時段。	I'll take that one.
好的，小姐。	Okay, ma'am.
你今天的髮型師是珍妮。	You will be seeing Jenny today.
哦，我喜歡珍妮。	Oh, I like Jenny.
那很好。	That's good.
你可以先進去洗頭。	You can go get your shampoo.

| 好的，謝謝你。 | That would be good. Thanks. |

Unit 3

結帳和付小費

Dialog 1

謝謝你。我很喜歡。	Thanks. I enjoyed that.
哦，不用客氣。	Oh, you're welcome.
你做得很好。	You did such a good job.

我會給你不少小費。	I'm gonna give you a hefty tip.
剪頭髮是十二美元。	The price of the haircut is 12 dollars.
這裡有十五塊。	Here's fifteen dollars.
不用找零錢了。	Keep the change.
謝謝你。	Thanks.

Dialog 2

別隨便把小費全部在一個地方花光噢。	Don't spend it all in one place.
請再光顧。	Come back soon.
哦，別擔心。	Oh, don't worry.
我總喜歡來你們這兒。	I often like to visit you.
那很好。	That's great.

| 祝你愉快。 | Have a nice day. |
| 你也一樣。 | Same to you. |

hefty
['hɛftɪ]
相當多的

tip
小費

change
零錢

spend
花錢

Chapter 18

社交英語

Unit 1

生日

Dialog 1

瑪麗，祝妳生日快樂。	Happy birthday, Mary.
謝謝你。	Thanks.
妳今天幾歲？	How old are you today?
十九歲。	Nineteen.
算了吧。	Come on.
妳女兒都已經十九歲了。	Your daughter is 19.

女人是從來不透露她真實年齡的。	A lady never reveals her true age.

嗯，妳看起來的確年輕。	Well, you sure do look young.
我知道。	I know.
我想我可以姑且相信妳是十九歲。	I guess I could believe you're 19.
真的嗎？	Really?
不，不是真的。	No, not really.
那我看起來像幾歲？	Then how old do I look?

vocabulary

reveal [rɪˈvil]		透露
lady		女士
age		年紀
look		看起來

Unit 2

婚禮

Dialog 1

這間教會很漂亮，不是嗎？	Isn't this a beautiful church?
嗯，它不像教會，倒像間小禮拜堂。	Well, it's not so much the church as it is this chapel.
是啊，妳說得對。	Yes. You're right.
這些花使這個小禮拜堂看起來真的很好看。	The flowers really make it look gorgeous.
我喜歡那些蠟燭。	I love the candles.
哦，音樂開始了。	Oh, the music's starting.
新娘進來了。	There's the bride.
該站起來了。	Time to stand up.

哦，她真的好美啊。	Oh, she's absolutely breath-taking.

Dialog 2

瑪麗，恭喜妳辦了這麼一個接待會。	Congratulations on pulling off the reception, Mary.
相信我，很不容易的。	It was hard, believe me.
妳家真漂亮。	Your home is so beautiful.
為了珍的婚禮，花了很多功夫去做的。	Well, it took quite a bit of work to do all this for Jane's wedding.
我想像得到。	I can imagine.
過去六個月我一直在清洗，又把雜物分類。	I've been cleaning and sorting junk for the past six months.

vocabulary

chapel [ˈtʃæpl̩]	小禮拜堂
gorgeous [ˈgɔrdʒəs]	（口語）極好的

bride [braɪd]	新娘
absolutely [ˈæbsəˌlutlɪ]	非常
breath-taking	很漂亮
reception [rɪˈsɛpʃən]	接待會
wedding [ˈwɛdɪŋ]	婚禮
sorting [sɔrtɪŋ]	分類（sort的現在分詞）
junk	（口語）各類雜物

Unit 3

宴會

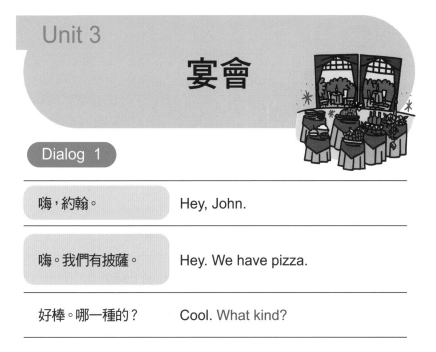

Dialog 1

嗨，約翰。	Hey, John.
嗨。我們有披薩。	Hey. We have pizza.
好棒。哪一種的？	Cool. What kind?

一個是香腸，另一個是漢堡。	One's sausage, the other's hamburger.
好好吃哦。我肚子餓了。	Yummy. I'm hungry.
別客氣，你儘管拿。	Help yourself.

Dialog 2

你有沒有什麼飲料可以喝的？	Do you have anything to drink?
你有沒有帶禮物來送我？	Did you bring me a present?
幹嘛？	Why?
開個玩笑而已。	Just kidding.
你有沒有可樂？	Do you have coke?
有，我們還有啤酒呢！	Yes. We also have beer.

vocabulary

pizza [pɪzɑ]   披薩

sausage [ˈsɔsɪdʒ]	香腸
hamburger [ˈhæmˌbɝgɚ]	漢堡
present [ˈprɛzn̩t]	禮物
beer	啤酒

Unit 4

邀請

Dialog 1

嗨，約翰。	Hey, John.
什麼事？	What?
星期五在我們家有個宴會。	There's a party at my house Friday.
妳父母到外地去了？	Parents out of town?
是的，宴會七點開始。	Yeah, it starts at 7.

好棒，我會來參加。	Cool, I'll be there.

Dialog 2

嗨，瑪麗。	Hey, Mary.
嗨。	Hey.
你星期五要來我家嗎？	Do you want to come over Friday?
我們有一個宴會，有披薩和電影。	We're having a party- pizza and movies.
聽起來好像不錯，什麼時候？	Sounds cool, what time?
八點鐘。	Eight o'clock.
我會去。	I'll be there.

vocabulary

party	宴會
parents	父母

Unit 5

拜訪

Dialog 1

約翰開門……

嗨，請進來。	Hi, come on in.
謝謝你。	Thanks.
這是我的新公寓。	This is my new apartment.
哇，看起來很好耶。	Wow, it looks nice.
謝謝你。	Thank you.
不用客氣。	You're welcome.

Dialog 2

這個公寓住得怎麼樣？	How is it working out for you?

哦，非常棒。	Oh, it's fantastic.
這個公寓很方便。	This apartment is so convenient.
真的嗎？	Really?
是啊，離網球場只有幾步路。	Yes. It's just a few yards from the tennis court.
你這兒有網球場？好棒！	You have a tennis court? Cool!
還有一個很好的俱樂部哪。	There's also a really nice clubhouse.

vocabulary

apartment [ə'pɑrtmənt]	公寓
fantastic [fæn'tæstɪk]	極棒的
convenient [kən'vinjənt]	方便的
yard	碼
tennis court	網球場
clubhouse ['klʌbˌhaʊs]	俱樂部

Unit 6

恭喜

Dialog 1

約翰，恭喜你結婚。	Congratulations on your marriage, John.
謝謝你。	Thank you.
謝謝你來參加。	Thanks for coming.
哦，我好喜歡那場婚禮。	Oh, I loved the ceremony.
謝謝。	Thank you.
記得告訴你的新娘子，說我衷心祝福她。	Be sure to tell your bride best wishes.
我會的。	I will.

約翰，恭喜了。	Congratulations, John.
謝謝你。	Thanks.
大學畢業的滋味怎麼樣？	How does it feel to be a college graduate?
感覺挺好的。	It feels good.
現在我期盼把大學貸款給還清！	Now I can look forward to paying off all those college loans!
哦，是啊。要還貸款真令人討厭。	Oh, yeah. That stinks.
不錯，但我的大學教育是值得的。	Yes, but my college education was worth it.

vocabulary

congratulations	[kən͵grætʃə'leʃənz]	恭禧
marriage		婚姻
ceremony	['sɛrə͵monɪ]	儀式
graduate	['grædʒʊ͵et]	畢業生
loan		貸款
education		教育

Chapter 19

旅行社

....

Unit 1

詢問

Dialog 1

我想知道一套蜜月旅行的行程,價錢是多少。	I need to find out what the rates are for honeymoon packages.
我們有各種不同的行程安排。	We have several different varieties of packages.
你的預算是多少?	How much do you want to spend?
我還不太確定。	I'm not sure.
但是我未婚妻想要去維京群島。	But my fiancee wants to see the Virgin Islands.

那是一個很明智的抉擇。	That's quite a good choice.
那些島嶼真的很漂亮。	They're really beautiful.
我們打算停留五天四夜。	We want to stay for about 5 days and 4 nights.
或者更久一點，但是要在不同的島嶼。	Or maybe longer, but on different islands.

Dialog 2

在每個島上過三個晚上怎麼樣？	How about 3 nights on each island?
那聽起來很好。	That sounds good.
包括些什麼？	What is included?
包括三餐，旅館，娛樂，飲料，跳舞，還有最多達五百元的紀念品。	Meals, room service, recreation, drinks, dancing, and souvenirs up to $500.

總共是多少錢？	How much does that cost?
一千九百九十九美元。	$1999.00.
那聽起來非常划算。	That sounds like a smashing deal.
我就要那一個！	I'll take it!

vocabulary

rate [ret]		價格；費用
honeymoon [ˈhʌnɪˌmun]		蜜月
package [ˈpækɪdʒ]		整套旅行安排
varieties [vəˈraɪətɪz]	各種不同的（variety 的複數）	
fiancee [fiˌɑnˈse]		未婚夫
choice [tʃɔɪs]		選擇
island [ˈaɪlənd]		島嶼
included [ɪnˈkludɪd]	包括（include 的過去分詞）	
recreation [ˌrɛkrɪˈeʃən]		娛樂
souvenir [ˌsuvəˈnɪr]		紀念品
smashing [ˈsmæʃɪŋ]		（口語）極好的

安排旅遊

Dialog 1

好，我們需要你填一些表格。	Okay, we need to have you fill out some forms.
你可以給我看你的信用卡嗎？	May I see your credit card?
如果你真的想看的話，可以。	Only if you really want to.
我才並是不真的要看呢。	I don't really want to.
那你是在開玩笑囉。	You must be kidding.
我被你打敗了。	You must be smart.
是用Visa卡嗎？	Will this be Visa?
不，是Master卡。	No, Master card.

你在填這些表格的時候，我可以告訴你有關這個旅行安排的娛樂部份嗎？	While you're filling out those forms, may I tell you about the recreation part of the package?
兩件事同時做，我沒辦法專心。	I can't concentrate on two things at once.
嗯，那麼，我只要你聽就好。	Well, then, I'll just ask you to listen.
你這個人硬是說一不二噢。	You're very assertive.
你這個人卻是人家肚裡的蚵蟲噢。	You're very perceptive.
還是跟我講講這個旅遊吧。	Tell me about the tours.

fill out
填寫

form
[fɔrm]
表格

credit card
信用卡

smart
聰明的

recreation
[ˌrɛkrɪˈeʃən]
娛樂；消遣

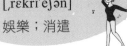

concentrate
[ˈkɑnsn̩ˌtret]
專心

at once
同時／立刻

assertive
[əˈsɝtɪv]
很堅持的

perceptive
[pɚˈsɛptɪv]
知道人家在想什麼的

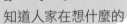

Chapter 20

生病

Unit 1

頭痛；感冒

Dialog 1

我的頭好痛。	I have such a bad headache.
你要吃阿斯匹靈嗎？	Do you want aspirin?
不要，阿斯匹靈會使我的胃不舒服。	No, aspirin upsets my stomach.
這樣你還要吃嗎？	Do you want to take it anyway?
不，我只要疼痛藥 Tylenol。	No, I only want Tylenol.
那，我沒辦法幫你忙。	Well, then I can't help you.

你星期二怎麼沒來上課？	Why did you miss class Tuesday?
我感冒了。	I had a cold.
感冒？	A cold?
那不成理由的。	That's no excuse.
我鼻塞好厲害，弄得我頭好痛。	I had such bad congestion that my head hurt.
是嗎？你錯過很精彩的一節課。	Well, you missed a really cool lecture.
李博士教了關於電腦病毒的東西。	Dr. Lee talked about computer virus.
整學期我就是在等這一個單元！	I've been waiting for that topic all semester!

Dialog 3

你應該來的。	You should have come.
那沒什麼關係。	It doesn't matter.

反正我一整堂課只會不斷擤鼻涕。	I would have been wiping my nose the whole time.
那有什麼關係。	So, big deal.
一堂課不過七十五分鐘而已。	It's only 75 minutes.
我可以抄你的筆記嗎？	Can I copy your notes?
可以。我想如果是我病了的話，你也會讓我抄你的筆記。	Sure. I guess you would let me copy yours if I were sick.
我當然會。	Of course I would.

vocabulary

headache [ˈhɛdˌek]		頭痛
aspirin [ˈæspərɪn]		阿司匹靈
upset		使不舒服
stomach		胃
cold		感冒
excuse [ɪkˈskjuz]		理由
congestion [kənˈdʒɛstʃən]		鼻塞
miserable [ˈmɪzrəb!]		很難受的

topic [ˈtɑpɪk]	題目
semester [səˈmɛstɚ]	學期
copy	抄
note	筆記

Unit 2

胃痛、嘔吐

Dialog 1

嗨，是約翰嗎？	Hi, John?
是的。	Yes.
我是瑪麗。	This is Mary.
我打電話來告訴你今天晚上我不能來。	I'm calling to say I can't come in tonight.
為什麼呢？	Why not?
我可能得了流行性感冒或是別的。	I have the flu or something.

昨天晚上我吐了。	I threw up last night.
盡量多休息，因為我明天真的需要你。	Try to get as much rest as possible because I really need you tomorrow!

Dialog 2

哈囉，是約翰嗎？	Hello, John?
是的。嗨，瑪麗。什麼事？	Yes. Hi, Mary. What's up?

我在想不知道你要不要打排球。	I was wondering if you wanted to play volleyball.
不行，我病了。	No, I'm sick.
我發燒，但覺得很冷，而且先前我還嘔吐。	I have a fever but I'm cold, and I threw up earlier.
哎呀，天啊。我希望你覺得舒服一點。	Oh, man. I hope you get to feeling better.
如果你能夠過來照顧我的話，我會覺得好一點。	I would feel better if you came over and took care of me.

flu	流行性感冒
threw up	嘔吐 （throw up 的過去式）
possible ['pasəbl̩]	可能的
volleyball ['valıbɔl]	排球
fever ['fivɚ]	發燒

Unit 3

拉肚子

Dialog 1

你準備好了嗎？	Are you ready yet?
是的。	Yes.
你怎麼這麼久？	What took you so long?
我在浴室裡拉肚子。	I was in the bathroom with the runs.
真噁心。是痢疾嗎？	Gross. Diarrhea?
沒有那麼嚴重。	It's not so bad.

好了，不管是什麼，我不要再聽了。	Okay, whatever, I don't want to hear about it.
你要耐著性子，而且試著放輕鬆地聽。	It's just that you have to be patient and try to relax.
夠了。	Enough.
我不想再聽任何有關你在浴室的事。	I don't want to hear any more about your bathroom time.
為什麼不要？	Why not?
哦，好了，我可以吃東西了。	Oh well, I'm ready to eat.
要是我們去餐廳，我還可以趕得及去洗手間，妳來點菜。	If we run to the restaurant, I can make it to the bathroom and you can order.
你確定要去？	Are you sure you want to go?
去洗手間？	To the restroom?
我可沒有選擇，非去不可啊。	I have no choice.

the runs	拉肚子
gross [gros]	好噁心
diarrhea [ˌdaɪəˈriə]	痢疾
patient [ˈpeʃənt]	有耐心的
relax	放輕鬆
restroom	洗手間

unit 4

宿醉

Dialog 1

從我昨天的宿醉醒來之後，我就一直有輕微的、討厭的頭痛。	Ever since I woke up with a hangover yesterday, I have had this subtle, annoying headache.
你宿醉？	You had a hangover?
我還以為你對宿醉有免疫力哪。	I thought you were immune to those.

我想要是我沒喝那麼多真正的烈酒，我是有免疫力。	I guess that's when I don't drink too much of one really nasty drink.
那是什麼酒？	What was that?
我們玩喝『白蘭地』的遊戲。	We played this game with brandy shots.
我討厭白蘭地。	I hate brandy.

Dialog 2

剛開始我以為我喜歡白蘭地。	I thought I liked it at first.
但現在我想我永遠都不再喜歡了。	But now I think I'll dislike it forever.
你覺得怎麼樣？	How do you feel?
就是頭痛、肚子餓，或許是胃也痛吧。	Just achy and hungry, or maybe my stomach just aches, too.
至少不是很嚴重的痛。	At least it's not a bad one.

你肯定不願親自體驗嚴重的宿醉是什麼樣子的。

You don't want to know what a bad hangover is.

hangover
['hæŋ,ovɚ]
宿醉

subtle
['sʌtl]
細微的

shot
（烈酒等的）一杯

annoying
[ə'nɔɪɪŋ]
惱人的

immune
[ɪ'mjun]
有免疫力的

nasty
['næstɪ]
猛烈的；難纏的

forever
永遠的

ache
[ek]
痛

租車

Unit 1

詢問

Dialog 1

嗨，有什麼事嗎？	Hi, how can I help you?
我想知道你們的價錢。	I want to know your rates.
那要看是什麼車來決定。	It depends on the vehicle.
我有公司折扣。	I have a corporate discount.
要什麼樣大小的車？	What size vehicle?
小型的汽車。	A compact car.

我們的週末優待價是六十九塊九毛五。	Our special weekend rate is $69.95.
一個週末是算幾天？	How long is that weekend?
如果你今天租車，你必須在星期天下午三點之前還車。	If you rent the car today, you must return it by Sunday at 3:00 p.m.
你們現在有什麼樣的小型車？	Which types of compact cars are available?
我們所剩下的就是三陽喜美。	All we have left is the Honda Civic.
好的，聽起來還可以。	Okay, that sounds good.

vocabulary

rate		價錢
corporate [ˈkɔrpərɪt]	形	公司的
discount [dɪsˈkaʊnt]		折扣
vehicle [ˈviɪkl̩]		車輛

compact [ˈkɑmpækt]　　　　　　（汽車）小型的

available [əˈveləb!]　　　　　　現成的；可得的

Unit 2

租車；還車

Dialog 1

我需要你填這張表格。	I need you to fill out this form.
好的。	Okay.
可以將你的信用卡給我嗎？	May I see your credit card?
在這兒。	Here.
好的，小姐。	Okay, ma'am.
總共是六十塊九毛五美元。	The total is $60.95.

會記到妳的Master卡帳上。	It's going on your Master Card.
是不限里程數嗎？	Do I get unlimited mileage?
是的，小姐。	Yes, ma'am.

Dialog 2

我來還我租的車子。	I am here to return the car I rented.
油缸是滿的嗎？	Is the gas full?
是的，我剛把它加滿。	Yes, I just filled it up.
好的。總共是六十塊九毛五。	O.K. The total is $60.95.
喏，這兒，六十塊九十五分。	Here. Sixty dollars and ninety-five cents.
謝謝。	Thank you.
你喜歡這部車嗎？	Did you like the car?

它帶我到我想去的地方，沒出差錯。	It got me where I needed to go.
我想也是。	I guess so.
有來回載送的車輛可坐到機場嗎？	Is there a shuttle to the airport?

終點

Dialog 3

來回載送的車輛在辦公室旁邊接你。	The shuttle picks you up right over there by the office.
它幾時會到？	When does it come?
哦，應該是隨時都會開回來了。	Oh, it should be back at any moment.
好。	Good.
謝謝你選擇『吉』租車公司。	Thank you for choosing Budget.
祝你愉快。	Have a nice day.
你也一樣。	Same to you.

unlimited [ʌnˈlɪmɪtɪd]	無限制的
mileage [ˈmaɪlɪdʒ]	里程
rented [ˈrɛntɪd]	出租（rent 的過去式）
full [fʊl]	滿的
fill up	把汽油加滿
shuttle [ˈʃʌtl̩]	來回載送的車輛

Unit 3

暈車

Dialog 1

媽，這部車子味道很難聞。	Mom, this car is so smelly.
不，不會。	No, it's not.
不要再抱怨了。	Stop complaining.

這部車子的味道令我想吐。	The smell of this car makes me nauseated.
我很抱歉。	I'm sorry.
你肚子餓了嗎？	Are you hungry?
是的。	Yes.
我們停下來找個地方吃東西。	Let's stop and eat somewhere.
你想要吃什麼，麥當勞嗎？	What do you want, McDonald's?

Dialog 2

我不知道。	I don't know.
我覺得不舒服。	I don't feel good.
那邊有一家『漢堡王』。	There's a Burger King.
我想要吃炸雞。	I want fried chicken.

我想這條路上不會有賣炸雞的餐廳。	I don't think there's a restaurant on this road with fried chicken.
肯德基炸雞店。	Kentucky Fried Chicken.
在哪裡？	Where?

smelly
['smɛlɪ]
有（難聞的）味道

nauseated
['nɔsɪ,etɪd]
想吐的

complaining
抱怨（complain的 名詞）

hungry
飢餓的

restaurant
['rɛstərənt]
餐廳

Chapter 22　坐公車

Unit 1　行車路線

Dialog 1

這部公車開往哪裡？	Where does this bus go?
你要去哪裡？	Where do you need to go?
去火車站。	To the railroad station.
那要搭326號公車。	That's the 326 route.
這是45號公車。	This is the 45 route bus.
是、是，很感謝。	Okay, thanks a lot.
祝你愉快。	Have a nice day.

Chapter 22

Dialog 2

嗨，這是326號公車嗎？	Hi, is this the 326?
是的，小姐。	Yes, ma'am.
妳要到哪裡？	Where are you headed?
中央圖書館。	The Central library.
有經過，小姐。	Yes, ma'am.
我會載妳到那裡。	I'll take you there.
謝謝。	Thank you.
不用客氣。	You're welcome.

vocabulary

railroad	鐵路
station ['steʃən]	站
route [raʊt]	路線
head	朝某個方向走
library	圖書館

Unit 2

找座位

Dialog 1

這個座位有人坐嗎？	Is this seat taken?
據我所知，沒有。	Not as far as I know.
那我可以坐這裡嗎？	Can I sit here?
請便。	Go ahead.
謝謝。	Thanks.
沒問題。	Sure.

Dialog 2

我可以坐這裡嗎？	May I sit here?

沒有其它的座位了嗎？	Aren't there any other seats?
恐怕沒有。	I'm afraid not.
好，讓我把我的袋子拿開。	Okay, let me move my bags.
我來幫你。	I'll help you.
行了。	There you go.

other
['ʌðɚ]
其他的

seat
[sit]
座位

bag
袋子

afraid
[ə'fred]
恐怕

232

Chapter 23　搭計程車

MP3-24

Unit 1

到哪裡？

| Dialog 1 | |

你要到哪裡去？	Where do you need to go?
到花旗銀行。	The Citibank.
好的，小姐。	Okay, ma'am.
把安全帶繫好。	Fasten your seat belt.
我很幸運招呼到你。	It's lucky that I found you.
你一直叫不到計程車嗎？	Have you had trouble finding a cab?

Chapter 23

不是的，你是第一輛。	No, you're the first one.
我立刻就招呼到你了。	And I found you right away.

Dialog 2

那你為什麼覺得幸運？	Then why do you feel lucky?
因為我很急。	Because I'm in a hurry.
大部份的人都急。	Most people are.
你急什麼？	What's your hurry?
我要即時趕到銀行去存款。	I'm trying to get to the bank in time to make a deposit.
那麼，我想你還要再搭車回來？	Oh, then I suppose you need a ride back?
不用。事實上，銀行辦完事之後我要到對街去跟一個人碰面吃飯。	No. Actually, after the bank I'm meeting someone for dinner just across the street.

fasten ['fæsṇ]	繫緊
lucky ['lʌkɪ]	幸運的
seat belt	安全帶
cab	計程車
trouble	困難
deposit [dɪ'pɑzɪt]	存款
ride	乘坐
actually ['æktʃʊəlɪ]	事實上

Unit 2

車資

Dialog 1

我們到了。	We're here.
總共是二十元。	That will be $20.00.
你收信用卡嗎？	Do you accept credit cards?

我只收現金。	Cash only.
怎麼會這樣，真令人失望。	That's disappointing.
好吧，反正我們來到銀行了，我想我可以再領現金。	Well, since we're at the bank, I guess I can get some more.
真方便！	How convenient.
錢在這兒。謝謝。	Here you go. Thanks.

Dialog 2

小姐，祝妳有個愉快的晚上。	You have a nice evening, ma'am.
你也一樣！	You too!
祝妳有個好的約會。	Have a nice date.
那不是約會，是我先生。	It's not a date, just my husband.
再見了。	Take care.

好的。	Okay.

accept
[ək'sɛpt]
接受

cash
現金

disappointing
[ˌdɪsə'pɔɪntɪŋ]
令人失望的

convenient
[kən'vinjənt]
方便的

date
約會

國家圖書館出版品預行編目資料

跟美國人學：食衣住行美語會話/施孝昌著. --
新北市：哈福企業有限公司, 2024.03
　面；　公分. --（英語系列；88）
ISBN 978-626-7444-01-6(平裝)
1.CST: 英語 2.CST: 會話 3.CST: 讀本
805.188　　　　　　　　　　113000843

免費下載QR Code音檔
行動學習，即刷即聽

跟美國人學：食衣住行美語會話
(附QR碼線上音檔)

作者／施孝昌 著
責任編輯／Vivian Wang
封面設計／李秀英
內文排版／林樂娟
出版者／哈福企業有限公司
地址／新北市淡水區民族路 110 巷 38 弄 7 號
電話／(02) 2808-4587
傳真／(02) 2808-6545
出版日期／2024 年 3 月
台幣定價／379 元 (附線上 MP3)
港幣定價／126 元 (附線上 MP3)
郵政劃撥／31598840
戶名／哈福企業有限公司
封面內文圖 / 取材自 Shutterstock

全球華文國際市場總代理／采舍國際有限公司
地址／新北市中和區中山路 2 段 366 巷 10 號 3 樓
電話／(02) 8245-8786 傳真／(02) 8245-8718
網址／ www.silkbook.com 新絲路華文網

香港澳門總經銷／和平圖書有限公司
地址／香港柴灣嘉業街 12 號百樂門大廈 17 樓
電話／(852) 2804-6687
傳真／(852) 2804-6409

email ／ welike8686@Gmail.com
facebook ／ Haa-net 哈福網路商城

電子書格式：PDF